BOUND BY LUST

BOUND BY LUST

BOUND BY LUST
ROMANTIC STORIES OF
SUBMISSION AND SENSUALITY

EDITED BY
SHANNA GERMAIN

FOREWORD BY
ALISON TYLER

CLEIS
PRESS

Published in the United States by Cleis Press, Inc., 2246 Sixth Street, Berkeley, California 94710.

Printed in the United States.
Cover design: Scott Idleman/Blink
Cover photograph: © Sie Productions/Corbis
Text design: Frank Wiedemann
First Edition.
10 9 8 7 6 5 4 3 2 1

Trade paper ISBN: 978-1-57344-792-8
E-book ISBN: 978-1-57344-804-8

Contents

FOREWORD

Lust knows not where Necessity ends.
—Benjamin Franklin

The bondage part comes naturally to me. I want my hands cuffed. I want my eyes blindfolded. I want the slippery vinyl corset cinched in place around my slim waist. Did someone mention fishnet thigh highs and a pair of glossy black boots with a chrome zipper up the side? Forget having my number dialed—you've got me tattooed on your bicep.

What's hotter than bondage?

That's where the lust comes in. See, being tied up by someone who knows every nuance of what I like tops everything I've ever done. (And those who have been playing along at home for the last two decades know that I've done a lot.)

Sure, there are the sudden-attraction aficionados who prefer a rough night with a stranger. Nothing wrong with that. But I want something more. I want to be with a man who understands how to take me right up to the precipice of pleasure, who will promise every night to push on my inner boundaries with his big, rough hands. I want him to display his tools of pain and sweetness and make me plead:

Oh, god. Yes. Please. Yes.

Then right when I'm licking my lips in preparation of maybe—just maybe—uttering my safe word, I want to be with a man who knows to pull back, to unwind, to recoil and start fresh.

"Bondage with Someone You Love"—there's a category of society that's just begging for its own Hallmark section. Thankfully, *Bound by Lust* is here with nineteen whip-smart stories to fill the need.

Your need. My need.

XXX,
Alison Tyler

INTRODUCTION:
THE TIES
THAT BIND,
THE HEARTS
THAT BEAT

I would love to be whipped by you, Nora love!
—in a letter from James Joyce to his beloved wife

In our culture, there is an overarching belief that dirty, kinky, and downright nasty sex and romance cannot coexist. Sure, you can have fantastic sex with the one you love, but it should be vanilla sex, gentle sex, the kind that is full of sweet whispers and soft caresses and glowing skin by flickering candlelight.

It's an age-old scenario, and one that's been ingrained in our understanding of the lust/love connection for so long that we've come to believe it. When it comes to love, we're supposed to choose the nice, respectful—if somewhat boring—boy over the rough-riding motorcycle man who makes our lust rev into high gear with little more than a look. Everyone knows you take the girl dressed in lace home to meet your mother, while you take the girl dressed in leather home to meet your toy box. The good girl gets the engagement ring. The bad girl gets bent over your knee, her skirt pushed up and her underwear pulled down, your hand pinkening the globes of her ass with every swat.

Madonna and whore. Bad-boy lover and sweet-guy husband. And never the twain shall meet.

Thankfully, there is no proof that true love and kinky lust can't go hand in hand. In fact, it doesn't take much digging to realize the opposite is true. For as long as there has been love, there have been delightfully dirty acts between those whose hearts are entangled. And while there's nothing wrong with "romantic" sex, most of us would readily admit that there's something super-hot about getting tied up, sucked off, or spanked bare-handed by the ones we love. Sometimes, it's love and trust that creates a safe space for the kinky desires to be played out. Other times, it's the shared love of kink that brings two (or more) hearts together.

The stories in *Bound by Lust* explore many of the ways that lust and love interconnect to create sex that's dirty, degrading, mind blowing, arousing, and, yes, sweetly romantic. In "Marcelle," Alana Noël Voth's gripping story of love and redemption, a man finds more than his heart's desire in the acceptance of the woman he loves, while the characters in Sommer Marsden's "Reclaiming Spring" discover that dominance and submission help them reclaim something very important: their marriage. And for the artist in Kristina Wright's "Brushstrokes," the safety of her love creates a way for her to give a new voice to her deepest desires:

> She wrote, "I can't say what I need." The words faded, each brush stroke becoming lighter until it was gone. "But I still need."
>
> "What do you need, Mai Ling?" he asked softly, his fingers pulling gently through her hair.

"Harder," she wrote.
He wrapped his fingers in the long strands of her
dark hair and pulled. "Like that?"
"Harder," she wrote, in thicker, darker letters.

Not all of the stories in the collection showcase the serious side of love and lust. A stop at the sex toy store in Andrea Dale's "A Few Things to Pick Up on Your Way Home" becomes a sensual trip through humiliation and desire, while the characters in Allison Wonderland's "Preference for Deference" bring a lighthearted humor to their deviant play. There are tales of rope bondage, public humiliation, proper training, and even puppy play. One submissive finds her inner dominant while bending her German lover to her will in "Eine Klein Spanking," while in "Slave Sister," a couple invites another woman to join their love, and lust, lives.

The stories in *Bound by Lust* are sweetly romantic, but they're also kinky, dirty, and full of delicious debauchery. They'll make your libido soar along with your heart, showing once and for all that kink and love are not separate entities. They are bound together by the finest ropes, by the tightest knots, by the lustful beatings of loving hands—and loving hearts.

Shanna Germain
Portland, OR

RECLAIMING SPRING

Sommer Marsden

It was that final puddle and the short slurping slide through the mud that did it. I stomped into the house and skidded into the kitchen.

"Problem?" Anthony asked, chopping onions. Something boiled on the stove, and the windows were fogged from steam inside and cold air out.

"I hate spring," I seethed.

"Come on, now. Hate?"

A rage so swift and big flared up in me I bit my tongue. I pried off one orange rain boot and threw it at the small mat we kept by the kitchen door. What felt like tears pricked my eyes, and my throat narrowed with mystery emotion.

"Yes, hate."

"You don't hate spring," he said softly and continued his meticulous chopping.

"I do," I said. Angry that he would counter me on my own feelings. Livid that I had to explain my feelings to him—to anyone.

"No you don't."

"Anthony—"

He turned to me full-on. His hulking frame and dark hair shot with bits of silver filled my field of vision. "You don't hate spring."

The anger was so big in me—out of nowhere—it had teeth and claws, and it raged at his calm, even tone. "I do hate spring!" I spat. Thinking somewhere in me that this was possibly the most asinine fight we'd ever had. But even as I pondered it, my hand acted of its own accord, and the other orange rain boot went flying. Right at him.

He plucked it from the steamy air with one big hand, and his face barely changed. He simply set the boot down on the yellow tile floor and said, "Get downstairs, Kate."

"I—"

"Move," he said. He made a shooing motion with his hands like I was a mouse in his kitchen or a dust bunny on his dirty floor.

"No."

"Go, Kate. Downstairs. Now."

"No. I won't go downstairs now. This isn't the bedroom. You don't get to tell me what to do or paddle me or any of that shit. You don't get to tell me I don't hate spring or that my feelings are wrong or that I'm not having them!" I roared, and for the first time in ten years of marriage, I took a swing at my husband.

And there he was, unflappable Anthony, catching my hand, dipping his big body and coming up under my torso to lift me off my feet. He caught me up in that firm fireman's carry, turned the stovetop burner to simmer, and waltzed me across the kitchen floor.

"Put me down," I growled.

"You don't hate spring, Kate. You hate what it stands for. That's when you ended things with him." And then he was clomping down the basement steps with me over his shoulder—dumbfounded and still with the force of his words.

I was grieving for Kevin. For the end of an affair.

There had been a bad patch for our marriage. A year of turmoil—an inability to conceive and start the family we wanted. And then we turned on each other as if blaming the other would soothe the ache. Anthony had picked his poison—crowded bars and too much beer and booze. Mine had been the cool white sheets of another man. But there had come a point when we needed to decide—marriage or divorce. Choose one. Choose now.

We'd chosen each other, and I had ended it.

I was mourning Kevin, I thought again, and when Anthony opened the back door to our tiny fenced-in back yard, my head rapped the lip of the doorway. The blow was short and not too hard at all, but tears sprang to my eyes instantly as if waiting for an excuse.

I started to cry for real.

"It's okay. We'll fix it." Anthony always saw things linear. We would fix my pain over having lost my lover. I had cheated on him with a man; he had cheated on me with booze. But we would fix it. There was no question.

"I'm crying because you hit my head."

"No you're not," he said and set me on the picnic table like his overgrown doll.

"Yes, I am," I said with no real heat.

He put his finger under my chin and tilted my head so I had to look at him. "No. You're not. Now put your arms up over your head, Kate."

"What? Why?"

"Because my wife, we are reclaiming spring."

"I...what?"

I felt off-kilter and out of control and I didn't like that. We had our little sex games. Paddles and bondage here and there, power plays and some teeth marks on occasion. But this was in our backyard, and I had real anger, real sadness. He should be jealous and enraged. Instead he said again, "Put your arms up over your head."

I stared into his stormy eyes—the grey of an overcast October day—and I decided to listen. I put my arms up over my head.

He nodded once, bent and kissed me on the lips. Not a peck but not a proper kiss, either. I sat, transfixed, confused, exhausted as he tied my hands with laundry line looped over the beams of our deck that hung over our heads. This was the little shielded bit of the yard, under the deck but looking out over the expanse of the yard. We sat here at the picnic table in the summer and watched the rabbits come out hesitantly from under the shed.

Once he had me tied so that my arms had a bit of slack but not enough to put them down, he unbuttoned the top four buttons of my blue thermal T and popped my bra open. My breasts bounced free, pink nipples pebbled from the chilly air.

"Now you stay here while I finish the soup. And think about what you want. Do you want to let it go, or do you want to keep that anger and hurt and our mistakes alive?" Then he dipped his head and sucked first one nipple and then the other.

I felt the tug and thump of arousal mixed with some melancholy flex in my belly and lower in my cunt. For once I kept my mouth shut as he went back inside, the door banging and his bare feet whispering on the red linoleum stairs as he went back up to his pot of soup.

"Well, fuck," I said to the misty rain.

I looked at the grass—so green it seemed neon—and tried to remember the very brief good-bye that I had shared with Kevin. More of a dismissal if you had to know. But it had hurt, more than I had realized, until I found myself crying for no fucking reason. Or yelling. Or a combo deal that scared everyone but me. Kevin and his cock and the sweet dirty way he talked to me when he fucked me had been a lifesaver during my pain. His arms around me while my husband drank away his pain at some crowded bar had been solace—false solace—but at that point I'd have taken any kind of solace at all.

"This is stupid," I said, coiled there on the picnic table with my arms tied. Some blonde bird of prey who couldn't take flight but couldn't fully roost.

I didn't want to be aroused. And I didn't want to admit he was right. I certainly didn't want him to come and fix this for me—with me. But as I sat there, waiting, heart pounding—I realized I was wet. And not just from the misty rain. I was wet between my legs with the tight swollen feel of arousal.

"Damn."

"Who ya talking to, babe?"

I gasped, sounding stupid and girlish, but even I could hear the lust in that one little sound.

"You know," Anthony said, advancing on me. "It really gets me hot, the thought of you twisting here in the wind like this. At my mercy."

I made a sound in my throat I wasn't anticipating, and he smiled at me.

"Let's see if you like it too." He unbuttoned my jeans and dragged down the zipper. I watched his hands as if I'd never seen them before. Anthony pushed my waistband down just a bit so that he could slide his fingers into my panties. His fingertip found me, parted me, entered me. "Yep, you like it too. Don't you?"

I refused to answer, biting my lip. He kissed me and turned his back to go.

"Where are you going!" I blurted, ashamed to hear how eager I was. But now my pussy was truly humming with arousal, and he was leaving me?

"Gotta get the carrots in or they won't get soft. And nothing ruins a good rainy-day soup faster than hard carrots."

"I...oh." I would not beg. I clenched my jaw and kept my mouth shut as he went back in the house.

Fuck.

I remembered the good-bye fuck. Kevin had cried. I had hated him for crying. His tears had sealed my guilt deep inside of me, and for that I'd never forgive him. I didn't wish him ill, but I wanted him excised from my fucking mind—cut out of my memory like a tumor.

I tested my ties, and my arms sang with the pain of immobility. An ache that thumped in time with my heart had taken up residence just below my shoulder blade. It felt like someone had inserted a blade in there and was twisting it.

I moved a bit to the left, wishing without realizing it that Anthony could pull this off. That melting snow and misty rain and mud wouldn't make me feel rage and guilt and sadness. That when I listened to the drip-drip-drip of melting snowbanks I would only think of him—of him fucking me—of us.

The backdoor squeaked and I froze. "How is she? Is she simmering?" he asked over my shoulder, pressing his lips to the back of my neck, cupping my goose bump-studded breasts in his hands. "Lift your hips."

Because I wanted him to succeed, I obeyed. I rose up on my knees a bit and let him shimmy my jeans down over my hips. He tugged my legs back so that they came off the picnic table and I had to stand. Belly pressed to the wooden lip of the table, arms tied to the beam overhead, husband crowding in on my back. He gripped my hips, pushed the silken head of his cock to my hole, and waited.

I wanted to beg, but that guilt flashed in me again. The guilt of hurting not one man, but two, so I didn't deserve to beg.

"You have to let it go," he said, picking through my mind, it seemed. And then he thrust and entered me.

My toes hovered over the concrete patio, my shoulders screamed, and I embraced the pain. My penance. The pain would wipe the slate clean. The pleasure would bond me and Anthony again so that nothing would come between us again. Even our own grief.

He thrust, and I sighed and surrendered. And then he pulled out, kissed the back of my neck, and left.

Okay, this time I started to cry.

"He says I have to let it go," I told the laundry line conversationally. I watched rain whip the dogwood in the back of the yard. Tiny buds had started to appear on her branches. New life. New chances.

I remembered the good-bye fuck again and how Kevin had held me while I cried. How he hadn't held my desertion against me. And then how I had simply dismissed him. As if it didn't matter. It had mattered, though, and it had hurt ever since.

"I let you go. I wish you well. I'm sorry," I said to the green-green grass. "I fucked up and so did Anthony but we can fix it. We can."

I heard the back door slip open and felt him there, but I didn't turn. I waited to see what he would do, what he would say. His touched my shoulder, still warm under cotton thermal because only my breasts were exposed, and then he bent me just a bit at the waist so my belly brushed the ragged edge of the picnic table. He slipped back into me, holding my hips with his big hands like they were made of glass.

"I love you, Katie." He moved and my body responded, plump and swollen with arousal.

I could only nod, unable to speak from the unshed tears clogging my throat.

He moved a bit faster, and my body rode up to meet him, my upper thighs scraping the table lip, my mouth working but no sound coming out.

"Say you love me, too," Anthony said, reaching around me, finding my clit and giving it firm wet rubs with his rough fingertip.

"I love you. I do." And then the sob broke free, but Anthony drove into me and the sob became a cry as I came, my body flickering around him. The rain picked up, beating down out of the leaden sky. Drips snaked through the cracks of the deck and baptized us with cool wetness.

I pushed back to him, opening for him, wanting him to come too. He held me in his hands and stilled my hips as he disengaged.

"Oh, come on—"

"Hush," he said and walked to the front of me. Anthony nudged the picnic table away with a bump of his hip, and it groaned across the concrete as it slid.

He palmed my ass and lifted me a few inches. I wrapped my legs to his waist as his cock found me, slid home—spearing the wet slit of my pussy. My fingers found the overhead beam, and I wrapped my hands around it to hold myself up a bit, the biting clothesline no longer gnawing at my flesh.

We were face to face, lips to lips, his breath on my cheek. His eyes half-open and startling grey, his face set in a determined way. I held on tight to him with my thighs as he fucked me, driving deep, his mouth pressed to mine. His cock nudged all the places deep inside that made me shiver and say silent prayers to go faster, deeper, harder.

"You're mine again. All mine and no one else's."

"Yes."

"And I'm all yours, baby. Like it or not."

"Yes."

A fat drop of rain hit my forehead, streaked a cold trail over my eyelid, and fell away. More rain slipped through the deck as the storm raged out in the open, crashing into the new grass, making mud. Making a mess. Washing away the old.

"Spring is good." He grinned, leaned in, and bit my throat.

I nodded and felt my body grow tight around him.

"Spring is really good." His voice a soft murmur.

I leaned in and licked him, kissed him, put my mouth on him wherever I could. One of his hands broke free from my ass and found my nipple, pinching hard the way I liked, driving a tiny spike of pain through my body. My fingers sang from holding me up, my pussy thumped with a fresh need for release, and when my husband pinched me once more I tossed my head back and cried out under the steady hiss of rain—coming hard. Surrendering.

Anthony came with a small grunt and then uncoiled the rope that held me. He sat back on the picnic table with me still wrapped around him—my arms around his neck, my legs around his waist. God, I hope no one could see us down here. But if they could—fuck it.

I felt his heartbeat slow, and mine followed suit. He stroked my hair. "There's soup."

I shivered.

"It's warm inside."

"I know."

A huge drop of rain fell and smacked me in the forehead, but my gaze was trapped on the bright green lawn and the falling rain. Anthony chuckled and brushed it away. "That one got you good."

"It's okay," I said, squeezing him with my whole body. "I like it."

BEING HIS BITCH

Janine Ashbless

The theme for the Club Night this month was "The Pet Show."
There was no way that Dev and I were going to miss this
one, and we put a lot of effort into my costume—or rather, lack
of costume, since it was nearly all body paint. I picked the color
scheme based on a boxer dog that lives down our street: cream
belly and chest, but a beautiful dark brindle all over the back
and legs and face. I had my hair cut short and elfin and made a
pair of dog ears in velvety faux fur that sat atop my head, half-
pricked and endearingly floppy. Dev did the paintwork himself,
using a skin-friendly, grease-free ink; he's in graphic design, and
he loves to get his art kit out when he has an excuse to do something properly creative.

The airbrushing took a couple of hours, there were so many
layers. "It ought to last out the night, unless you rub it off," he
said. But I wasn't making any promises.

To finish off my costume, we had a dog collar—a broad
greyhound one that made me hold my head up, with a dog

tag dangling from it—and a chain leash with a leather loop. Engraved on the disc was the legend "Naughty Little Bitch." We could've got that done discreetly ourselves, using one of those machines you find in pet stores, but Dev made me go into the engraver's shop and order it in person from the man behind the counter. The guy gave me one hell of a look but didn't ask any questions, and I emerged from the shop with my panties so wet and my legs so wobbly that I could hardly walk straight.

"All done?" Dev asked.

"Yes," I whispered, leaning my head against his chest.

He knew what that meant. Taking the disc from me with one hand, he put the other on my ass and gave me a squeeze and a pat. "Good girl." I whimpered and rubbed up against him, but he just chuckled. "Save it for Saturday night."

By Saturday I was strung out on anticipation and so inflamed with arousal that Dev had to order me to stop touching myself as we drove into the city. I shed my coat in the cloakroom with a feeling of profound relief.

Dev was wearing his favorite club costume: a kilt of thick industrial rubber, New Rock boots, and a steampunk top hat and goggles. He looked so good in that gear that I wanted to suck his cock already. I could see that quite a few people had turned up in some version of Furry costume, and I was sure I'd be a lot more comfortable than all of them in the heat of the rooms upstairs, but comfort wasn't what it was all about, here.

Dev clipped the leash to my collar and used it to pull me to him and plant a kiss on my lips, all slippery, possessive tongue, reminding me where my focus lay for the evening. "Ready?"

"Yes." Already people were checking me out, there in the lobby. I was aware of grins and raised eyebrows and nods. Under my paint I was naked and shaved as smooth as silk. I looked respectable from a distance but incredibly naughty close up, and that made my nipples stand out like switches ready to be flicked.

"I love you, Rosie," he growled. "So fucking much. You're so beautiful." Then he tugged the chain. "Heel, bitch."

We ascended the stairs slowly, morphing into character with every step, his pace proud and easy, my obedient place at his side and one step behind. Playing this particular game is, for me, the ultimate in intimacy. Playing it in public for the first time was taking our trust in one another to a whole new level.

We went into the bar first and queued so that Dev could order drinks—bottled beer for him, bottled water for me. As soon as he stopped walking I sank to my knees by his leg, waiting patiently as a good dog should. We had considered my staying on hands and knees throughout the night but had decided it would be irritatingly slow to move around, not to mention painful for me and not in a good way. Going to dog height when we were stationary seemed the best compromise.

"Hello Dev." Black leather chaps loomed over me. It was Bill, a club friend and someone we had played with before, but I didn't try to greet him. I was being a mute animal, after all. "Nice dog you've got there."

"Thank you."

"What's her name?"

"Princess."

"May I stroke her?" Etiquette is everything at the club. People are scrupulously respectful of boundaries: without that the whole thing would fall apart.

"Go ahead. She likes having her chest rubbed." Dev turned away slightly to give his order to the barman, and Bill stooped to scratch me gently behind the ears—my real ears.

I opened my mouth, panting a little and leaning into the caress. It was stuffy down here among the forest of legs. I could smell leather and spilt beer. The front of my admirer's pants was tented by a bulge, but that didn't mean anything in particular: most of the guys here walk round with a semi the whole night, and I can't speak for all the girls, but my pussy is open and juicy and fluttering from the moment we walk in. Bill crouched to caress the smooth cream blaze of my chest, stroking my breasts, and I shut my eyes in pleasure, pushing those orbs up into his hand. *I'm a dog. Anybody may stroke me, so long as my master gives permission. Anybody.*

"Good girl, Princess," he murmured. His fingers flicked my pert nipples. "You like that, don't you?"

I didn't answer, but as Dev turned back to us and Bill stood to talk to my owner once more, I caught the tips of his fingers with my tongue and licked them, and he laughed.

Carrying both drinks, Dev walked me though the rooms of the club—the dance floor, the theatre, the playroom where the keenest members were already warming up with floggers and paddles on the various pieces of equipment—and into the lounge. This has comfortable chairs and cushions, and there were plenty of people standing and sitting about, talking and showing off their costumes. I couldn't help looking furtively around, though my attention was supposed to be on Dev. They looked so beautiful, in their way. Not everyone had stuck to the Pet Show theme; it wasn't compulsory, so long as you wore something fetish. But many had. Cats and dogs mostly, though there was one woman in full pony-girl tack, including a small cart, and I've no idea how she and her driver had managed to get that up the stairs. A couple of kittens stopped their tussling to hiss at me as I walked past, and I rose to the challenge and barked excitedly in response, causing Dev to tow me away by my collar. As we retreated to the far side of the room, I saw one kitten pin the other and begin to give her a good licking.

Being surrounded by others with the calling to kink made my heart swell with awe and my sex ache. I could feel my libido slip free of its constraints and start to soar.

We met another couple we knew quite well. Annie, normally a carefully preened platinum blonde, was all in Dalmatian spots tonight, and she carried a rag rope between her teeth. As our two owners stood and watched, Annie and I had a tug-of-war game with the rope on hands and knees, jumping on each other and mouthing excitedly as we wrestled for the toy. That was fun: naughty fun, what with hands and mouths and bare bodies rubbing all over each other, but just plain childish fun too. There is such a lack of inhibition in being a dog, a simple innocence that still has room for sex. Annie nipped me on the ass until I squealed and rolled over in submission, surrendering her prize.

Annie's owner took her away toward the bar, the rope held triumphantly in her mouth, as I sat up panting. At that moment another dog came bowling in on all fours, his leash flying behind him. He bounced up and down around me, tongue lolling and ears flopping wildly, while I tried to stifle my giggles. Unlike me, he wore a tail: a stiff curl that rose from the butt-plug planted between his ass cheeks and waved with every step. I recognized him too; he was a well-known TV comedian. We sometimes get famous faces here, but discretion is also part of the rigid etiquette. Spinning top to tail, he made a show of sniffing my behind. I obliged, as dogs do, standing foursquare and then nudging his flank with my nose. Underneath the pale skin of his belly, his latex codpiece was stretched by his jutting stiffy. I stooped and gave the shiny rubber a little lick—just before Dev pulled me away.

"Get off!" he ordered, amused. "You filthy dogs!"

The comedian grinned, panting—and then bounded away as a woman rushed up waving a rolled-up newspaper. "Fido!" she snapped, grabbing his leash and swatting his ass good and hard. He howled in happy self-pity. She looked over her shoulder at Dev. "I'm so sorry! Has he been bothering your bitch? He's such a bad dog: he won't obey a word I say!"

"No problem," grinned Dev. "Just keep him away from the cats."

The naughty dog decided that sounded like a great idea and, spotting the pretty kittens on the far side of the room, set off determinedly toward them, yipping and towing his mistress. I had to cover my mouth with my hand to hide my giggles.

"Okay," said Dev. "I think we need to calm down."

I tried to look contrite as he led me to a chair in a corner. Sitting, he stretched his legs out in front of him and crossed his ankles. I took up my customary position straddling his shins, my head on his lap. I love Dev, but when I'm being Princess I love him even more, with a dog's unstinting trust and devotion. My pussy rested comfortably on the jut of his booted foot, my bare ass pointing at the world. Dev sipped his beer and watched me, his gaze sliding over the curves of my shoulders and waist and butt, over my spread thighs.

"Thirsty?"

I nodded. There was no rule against me talking, but silence helped me feel in character. Dev held the plastic glass of water to the level of my mouth and I lapped at it, grateful despite my awkwardness.

"You enjoying yourself, Princess?"

I smiled, my eyebrows telegraphing how much wicked fun I was having, and wriggled my bottom against the upper of his boot. The leather felt cool against my warm, wet pussy.

"Dirty little bitch," he murmured, pressing up into the concavity of my sex as his fingers tickled my neck and jaw. A chrome boot stud rubbed my clit, and I sighed with pleasure.

"You would have let that bad dog lick your ass, wouldn't you?"

I shrugged, teasing.

"You'd have let him mount you, dirty little bitch." His fingers stroked my throat, making me groan. I could feel the wet I was leaving on his polished leather.

Yes, maybe I would have. It's hard to think ahead when you're a dog; that's the master's job. I wasn't feeling at all responsible right now: I was aroused and completely surrendered to Dev's caressing fingers and pressing boot. Part of me was aware of the room around me, but only as a setting and a witness to my unashamed pleasure.

"Maybe I should find you a good stud dog."

Heat flooded my cunt, and I opened my eyes wide in alarm.

"We can probably do better than that silly mongrel." Dev set aside the drinks and reached to fondle my breasts. "What do you think, Princess?"

"Oh," I said, as he tugged my nipples, rolling and pinching them between his fingers. Hot lashes of sensation ran all the way down from his fingertips to my clit.

"Yes, I think that's a very good idea. A nice big stud dog to mate with my horny little bitch."

I met his gaze, my trepidation undisguised. We'd played with other people at the club, sure: I'd been spanked and scratched, groped and tickled. But that was all. It had never gone all the way. The thought of Dev picking someone to fuck me...

It made me burn and squirm and recoil and grind my hips.

"Which one shall I choose?" he whispered, sending shivers all over my painted skin. My heart was beating so hard he must have been able to feel it against his knee. "Something with a good pedigree. Something strong and fit and eager. With a nice big cock and fat, heavy balls. Something..." He lifted his face, looking out into the room. "What do you think?"

I craned my neck to see.

Oh *fuck*. It was Mistress Freda and her sub, Victor.

That thought was nearly enough to make me come there and then; a quivering spasm ran through me. Freda and Victor were a couple I'd had a crush on since we joined the club. So did everyone else, I think. They stand out in this crowd because they're black, but those two would stand out anywhere. They're both really tall and fiercely beautiful, and this night Freda was wearing a tight, boned pastiche of traditional hunting habit: a precariously low-cut red jacket and a miniature hat and veil, and shiny black boots with heels that could stake a vampire. Her long corn-rowed hair hung down her back in cords as tight and cruel as the lashes of a cat-o'-nine-tails. There was a riding crop holstered at her hip, and we were under no illusions that she knew how to use it. I've heard she's some sort of scary corporate lawyer.

I've no idea what Victor does for a day job, but he's built with the sort of hyper-real muscles you only see on sportsmen and in rap videos, and all of it was on show that night. His dress consisted mostly of leather strapping: one of those chest harnesses people put on bull terriers and mastiffs, with the legend "REX" printed down the breastbone, and a set of tack and metal rings around his ass and cock and balls that fully displayed his vital parts, flushed and swollen and ready. A glans-ring completed the "pet" theme: a chain led from it to Freda's elegant, nonchalant fingers.

"Whoa!" I moaned, forgetting myself. Dev chuckled.

It's not like we know Freda and Victor to talk to. She's a really haughty domme, and though she will deign to punish other people's subs sometimes, she plays too rough for most. I like a little recreational spanking, but they're in another league altogether. Victor likes *serious* pain. When the Club

Night theme was "Pirates," she'd tied him to a ship's wheel and whipped his back and ass raw with a leather strap, and he'd taken it without complaint. Groaned, sweated, clenched his teeth, yes—but taken it, and then got down to kiss her toes afterward and thanked her profusely.

"Hmm?" said Dev pointedly. "Would you like that, Princess?"

I tore my gaze from the other couple to meet his, biting my lip. My face was burning, my pussy melting. But I didn't say anything. I desperately wanted him to make the decision. He was the master, not me.

Dev lifted one eyebrow, and I felt his legs shift beneath me. "Sit, girl."

I moved back to sit on my heels, my heart pounding. He stood slowly, watching me with a critical eye.

"Legs open."

Obediently I spread my thighs.

"Now—stay." He let the chain leash slip from his hand to hang down between my outthrust breasts. The loop handle brushed my bare and sensitized mons, and I quivered inside. I watched him stroll away toward Mistress Freda, and I swallowed hard, trying to work moisture back into my nervous mouth. It all seemed to have drained down to my sex, which felt swollen and heavy.

This is real. Oh God—he's really going to ask. I'm a good dog. He'll look after me. I am doing as my master wants. I'm a good good dog.

He spoke to her. I watched the confident tilt of his shoulders and the easy nod of his head, gesturing back at me. I couldn't help admiring the sweep of his long kilt and the dull gleam of the rubber. Victor—or Rex—was kneeling quietly at his mistress's side, his neck turned so that he could look up at her with calm

devotion. The light glistened on his muscled chest: he was a
Rottweiler among toy poodles. When she glanced over at me, a
sharp sweet pain contracted inside my belly. I dropped my gaze
to the floorboards, too shy to meet hers.

Oh god. They were coming over. All three of them.

"Here she is," said Dev. How could he sound so calm?

"Hh," she grunted. "Kneel up straight." Obediently I hauled
my ass clear of my heels. The floorboards felt hard beneath my
knees. She hunkered down directly in front of me, and a casual
tug upon the cock-chain of her pet brought him to his knees
at her side. My vision was blurred, but I could see the morello
cherry glisten of her lips and the swing and bob of his turgid
length. She smelled expensive and wonderful. Slipping a hand
between my parted thighs, she explored my pussy. Her nails
were frighteningly long, but she was delicate, for which I was
grateful as her fingers slithered over my swollen folds, paddling
in the slick juiciness within. I was so wet that it was seeping
down the insides of my legs. When she stroked my clit with
one fingertip, a charge shot through me, and I couldn't help
whimpering.

"Yes, I think you're right: your bitch *is* in heat." Withdrawing
her hand, Freda held it up, glistening with my wetness. Her
nails were painted in red-and-black tiger stripes. Apex predator.
"Luckily for her I have the solution here."

Victor sniffed her proffered fingers, then licked them slowly
and lovingly. I could feel my thighs starting to shake.

"What do you think, Rex?" she purred. We all looked at
him. His answer was a great big piratical grin aimed straight at
me. My heart crashed wildly. I turned to Dev for reassurance,
cuddling up to his leg.

"She's a bit nervous, I'm afraid." He cupped my throat with
one hand and fondled my tit with the other.

"Young bitches often are, at first." Freda's smirk was wicked. "She'll learn to love it. Shall we?"

"Come on, Princess." Dev urged me to my feet and led me to the center of the room. There's a broad bench there, padded in red leatherette: a seat sometimes, but often a stage for whatever club members choose to display in public. I heard the room grow quieter as I climbed upon it, onto hands and knees, and Dev coaxed my thighs a little apart and my head up like I was Best of Breed at Crufts Dog Show.

Oh god. He's going to do it to me in public. They can all see my pussy now.

"My dirty little bitch," he murmured hoarsely, stooping to rub his face against mine. "Oh you dirty girl, you wonderful dirty girl."

I licked his lips.

Dev held my leash loosely as Freda led her pet round to my head. Standing, his cock was on a level with my mouth. His pubic hair was shaved down to a tight stubble, and his genitals, in their harness and rings, looked magnificent.

"Lick him," ordered Freda, tugging his cock on its chain and bringing him a step closer, right to my lips.

I was aware of people gathering around us to watch.

He had a truly beautiful cock, strong and straight and smooth, framed against thighs and a stomach like polished walnut. The glans-ring yanked it to full vertical, allowing me unrestricted access to the underside of the shaft and to his balls. That's where I started licking him. My mouth wasn't dry any more, but watering with hunger. He tasted good too— completely different from Dev, but just as yummy: masculine and musky with a hint of sandalwood soap. I could feel the heat surge through his shaft as I licked, filling it. He grunted in appreciation and pressed forward, rubbing his cock all over my face, hefting his scrotum so I could lick that too. I wasn't sucking tonight: dogs don't suck. I was all tongue as I worked my way from that big pouch hanging below, right up to the tip of his glans where a clear teardrop of pre-cum awaited me.

"Step back," said Freda, as it burned on my pouting lips. Victor shifted out of my reach, and she unclipped the chain from his glans-ring. The angle of his thick shaft didn't drop at all; he was at full and straining erection now. I heard a sigh of anticipation run through the circle around us. Dev ran his fingers down my spine. Reaching into the cleft of her awesome cleavage, Freda extracted a condom. She tore the wrapper open with her teeth, then skinned it onto her pet with swift grace and something near a flourish. Patting him on the ass, she instructed, "Take her, Rex."

He walked round behind me, harness jingling with each step. The crowd shifted, following him with their eyes, but I looked up at Dev. He cupped my chin in his hand. His eyes were shining, his throat glossed with perspiration. "Good girl."

I expected Victor to mount me straight away, but he put his big hands on my butt-cheeks and spread them. I knew my smooth pink crack and my flushed pussy were completely open to him. Then he took me by surprise, because he stooped and licked me, all the way up from my clit to my anus. I squealed and he did it again, burrowing his face in hard, sucking my swollen sex-lips, lapping and licking and slurping until I was dizzy with shock, then squirming his tongue into the tight clench of my back entrance. I'm a screamer: I can't keep quiet. I certainly wasn't quiet here. My squeals and cries rose like a musical scale. I arched my back and threw my head up and down. Yet in the middle of all that noise and chaos I felt completely safe, because Dev was holding my collar and keeping an eye on every move Victor made.

Only when he'd tasted me and opened me thoroughly did my big stud dog kneel up behind me on the leatherette and slap his cock against my pussy. I sank my shoulders down, presenting my ass good and high for him. His palm smacked my right butt-cheek with a crack like a starting pistol, and I felt his thick cock-head mash into the complex wetness of my sex. He pushed, trying to find an angle. But it took Freda's hands to guide him in, spreading my inner labia safely out of the target zone.

"Whoa," he said through gritted teeth; "you're tight, little bitch."

I groaned, half in pleasure, half in dismay.

"There," Freda chided, and reached underneath me. I felt her nails score my mons before her fingers settled on my clit. Oh, that felt good: that big cock inside my bitch cunt, and her expert caress on the button of my arousal. There was no more fear and no more discomfort, despite his considerable girth. Slowly at first, gaining confidence in my ability to take it, he powered into my slippery hole with thrust after thrust until his balls were slapping against my pussy. He filled me and reshaped me and gripped me tight, his fingers biting into my hips and ass, his thighs drumming against me. I could feel the whine of need inside me growing to a great howl.

Twisting, I rammed my head against Dev's pelvis, rubbing my face across his crotch. The thick rubber of his kilt stopped his erection from showing to the outside world, but I could feel the hard knot of his cock against my cheek. I licked at the rubber, tasting talc, panting.

"Please!" I squealed, forgetting my role. "Please!"

Suddenly galvanized, he tugged frantically at one buckled strap after another. Victor's cock was like a hammer pounding inside me. Dev made an opening big enough to pop his dick out into view, and I fell upon it with my mouth, sucking it deep into my throat. The more Victor thrust and Freda rubbed, the deeper I could take Dev. I didn't need to breathe. I didn't need to think. I only had one goal—and in minutes I was there. I screamed around Dev's cock as my orgasm exploded.

That was enough for Dev. He let loose down my throat, pumping his cream into me, filling my mouth so that I choked and snorted and guzzled it all down, like the greedy little bitch I am. Victor rammed harder and harder into the burning glow of my meltdown.

"Stop now," said Freda, stepping back. "Pull out."

Without hesitation, Victor pushed away from me, leaving a gaping void in my life.

"Hands behind your head."

I swallowed the last of Dev's cum and looked behind me, shocked. Victor stood with arms up, staring into space, his face twisted with frustration, his skin gleaming with sweat. He must have been right on the brink; his cock was a great glistening spear thrust out before him. But he was a true sub: far more obedient than any dog would have been.

"That'll do. Follow me." Freda looked over at Dev. "I hope his service satisfied."

"Very much so. Thank you." Dev was short of breath but admirably collected as he tucked his cock out of sight.

Freda nodded graciously and then turned away, unsheathing her riding whip. Victor followed in her footsteps as she led him toward the playroom and the punishment that was his reward. There was a scattering of nervous applause as the circle of watchers made way. Many moved to follow. They wanted to see.

I let my legs collapse under me. "Poor dog," I whispered.

"She wants him to last out the night." Dev bent and embraced me, sliding one arm beneath my thighs, plucking me from the bench. I curled up against his chest, licked his ear, then kissed him. I knew he liked to taste his own cum on my lips.

"I love you, Master."

"Was it good, Princess?"

"Very good, Master. Very very good. Thank you."

"You were fucking incredible. Just beautiful." He kissed my hair and carried me across the room, to the comfortable seat and the water I suddenly desperately needed. Snuggling up in his lap, I felt Dev's hand slip between my thighs, exploring the gape of my used sex. As he pressed my clit I groaned, shifting against him.

"What?" he growled. "More?"

"What does it say on my tag, Master? You know me."

"I do. You're my naughty little bitch."

"Yes Master." I brushed my lips against his. "All yours."

SPRING TRAINING

Donna George Storey

First Workout

I wish I'd never been with any other man but you."

"No, you don't."

Josh had a provocative habit of telling me what to think.

I rolled onto my stomach to look at him straight on. His eyes were a bewitching velvety brown, the lashes as thick as the ones you can buy at the drugstore.

"I do," I insisted.

"You don't," he repeated.

"I do. It's so damned hot with you. The others were just a waste of time. Pathetic, really, what I thought sex was."

He smiled. "See, you have a point of comparison. Otherwise, no matter how hot it was with me, you'd always wonder."

I snuggled close and rested my head on his shoulder. My hand wandered under the sheets to his thick cock, which was already stiffening for another inning of our double-header—an all-day fuckfest with stretch time for brunch and dinner. What else did we have to do on a stormy February Sunday?

"I really do wish I could wipe the memories clean away, not just from my mind, but from my body, too. Then you'd be my first and my best."

"I don't think that's possible," Josh said lazily. His hand had moved to my breast and was doing very pleasant things to my nipple.

My throat suddenly felt tight and dry. The way it always did when I was about to suggest we try something perverse in bed. "Maybe there is something we could do. Once...back in college...I let a boy come on my breasts, and he rubbed it all over. Then he wanted me to suck his fingers clean. He didn't even bother to make me come afterward. I still feel ashamed to think about that, but maybe if we do it the right way, with mutual pleasure, then I'll be free. Like a cleansing ritual."

Josh's fingers froze mid-pinch—had I shocked him?—but the way his cock twitched in my grip told me the idea turned him on, too.

After a long moment he said, "You know, Erin, I don't like to do things halfway."

I felt a funny, sexy flutter in my belly. "What do you mean?"

"I mean that there might be things we could do to wipe away those memories from your body. Or rather to train you so that every part of your erotic response belongs to me. But be fore-warned, if you consent to my spring training program, you'll never be able to go back to having sex with another man. No other hands, lips, or cock will ever fully satisfy you again."

I shivered at the finality of his words, but all the things he said would happen were already true. "Let's start right now."

He laughed. "Give me time to come up with my coaching

plan. Believe me, I'll be pushing you to the limit. But your intriguing proposal will be a fine warm-up for today. I will jerk off on your tits and smear my spunk all over, then make you clean me up with your tongue like a cat. And then I will most definitely make you come. But first you're going to suck me better than you've ever sucked a man before. You're going to take me deep into your throat to a place no dick has ever penetrated. Even if you're gagging, even if tears are streaming down your face from the effort, you're going to keep doing it, because you want me to own every inch of you."

Tears had already sprung to my eyes, but they had nothing to do with sadness or pain. My whole body was buoyed up with a feeling I could only describe as joy.

"Say you want to do it, Erin. That will be our contract."

"I want...I want every inch of my body to belong to you."

He jerked his chin downward. "Then let's get on with it."

Obediently I slithered under the covers and crouched beside his thighs. I'd never been so physically excited at the mere thought of taking a man into my mouth.

Suck me better than you've ever sucked a man before.

Pulse racing, my pussy juices coating my thighs, I opened my lips wide and bent to do his bidding.

I had a feeling it was only going to get better from here.

Week Three

The first Saturday in March found me sitting on Josh's cock, naked except for a Giants' World Series Champions baseball cap perched at a jaunty angle on my head.

"One, two, three, four, five...and release," he chanted.

I squeezed my secret muscles around him as hard as I could.

"Again," he said.

"I'm not sure I can keep doing this."

"Don't stop believing, Erin."

I took a deep breath and did another set, grimacing with the effort. He'd had me "working out" around his cock for ten minutes—butterfly flutters, progressive clenches, and now the extended holds. My whole lower half was pulsing and achy with lust.

But Josh apparently had his mind on my athletic development.

"We'll take a short break. Get some water."

I reached for the water bottle he had ready on his nightstand and sucked down a mouthful of cool liquid.

"You definitely feel stronger down there. Did you practice twice a day this week?"

"Yes," I answered proudly. "Even though you were on that business trip and neglected your girlfriend terribly."

"I'll make it up to you. But don't change the subject. Did you get sore?"

"Not as much as the first week."

He nodded smugly. "When we get you in proper shape, you'll have a brand new pussy. Strong and responsive and molded to my cock like it was custom made for me."

I giggled.

He tilted his head appraisingly. "So when you did your exercises while I was away, did you play with yourself afterward?"

My smile faded. I figured he jerked off when he was traveling, why couldn't I do the same? "Well, not every time."

"But sometimes?"

I nodded, but he didn't need to know the rest—that I actually succumbed to temptation every evening and most mornings.

Josh hooked his finger under my chin so I was forced to meet his eyes. "Don't misunderstand me. I like it that you're so horny you can't keep your fingers out of your panties. But I need to know—for training purposes—do you put something in your vagina when you masturbate?"

This was getting pretty personal. "Not often," I stuttered.

"What do you mean by that? Once a week? Once a month?"

I'd joked with guys about such things in the past, but I'd never talked so openly about the *details* before.

"Erin, come on. You're not just giving me your body. I want you to show me everything—your mind, your history, your fantasies."

"Well, I tried putting a...oh, god this is embarrassing...a zucchini inside a few times, but it felt too naughty. Like I might ruin myself or be imprisoned for abusing innocent vegetables." I gave him a mischievous smile.

But Josh was all business. "That's going to change. A pussy was made to be filled. From now on I forbid you to do your workout, or even more important, touch your clit in any way, unless you have something inside. A zucchini will do. No, I have a better idea. I want you to buy yourself a dildo. Six inches long—about my size—no monster that will stretch you out. And get something nasty with veins and a ball sac so that if someone finds it they'll know exactly what you do with it."

I flinched at his words but knew I would obey.

"I want you to carry it around in your purse at all times. You'll never know when I'm going to text you with an order to practice your exercises in the ladies' room at work. I want my assistant coach close at hand to help you."

"I don't think a dildo will fit in my purse," I protested weakly.

"Buy a bigger purse then. Okay, enough rest for the rookie. And put that cap on straight. Show respect for your organization."

"Yes, *Sir*," I barked out, grinning as I yanked the visor forward.

"I don't need any attitude, Missy, or you just might get cut from the team. Now squeeze me as fast and hard as you can, a sprint to home plate. *A-one and a-two....*"

Thus far, Josh had kept his hands chastely at his sides, but now he took one stiff pink nipple in each hand and twisted them between his fingers in time with my next contraction.

I shuddered as a jolt of pleasure shot through me. Instinctively I clamped down on him, rocking my hips lewdly. The pressure of his groin on my very swollen clit left me gasping.

"Is it okay if I, um, have an orgasm while I'm working out, Coach?" The word *coach* trailed off into a moan.

"It's more than okay, baby," he purred. Suddenly one nipple was swimming in the heat of his mouth, and he was tug, tug, tugging it with his lips, and I was sliding right into home plate, clit first, the howl tearing through my throat louder than the crowd at AT&T Park.

The start of spring training had indeed been tough, but I had to admit it was growing on me.

Week Four

My cell phone beeped discreetly. As I expected, it was a text message from Josh: "Xrcises at 3, send pic, CJ."

I glanced guiltily around my cubicle, not that anyone was likely to be spying on me. And if they were, they'd have no clue what had just transpired. But I knew well enough Coach Josh was instructing me to go to the ladies' room in twenty minutes, plough myself with his "assistant," snap a picture with my iPhone, and email the evidence to him post haste. *Not that I don't trust you,* he told me, *but I think you're ready for an exhibition. Besides, you've never sent pictures like this to another man, have you?*

I had to confess that I had sent someone a picture of my

tits once—what woman hasn't?—but never anything quite this risky. Yet somehow I trusted Josh. I caught myself shifting my weight in my chair. My panties seem to have bunched up in my slit, and the friction was highly distracting.

Could I make it all the way until 3:00?

I sat up tall in my chair and tried to focus on the report in front of me. Or more accurately, *failed* to focus on the report. All I could think about was how heavy and sensitive my breasts felt, how the fabric of my bra was chafing my nipples. And how my butt crack tingled expectantly, too, as if my back door remembered Josh's promise that next week we'd focus on anal sex of every variety.

The text on the screen before me began to swim.

The truth was Josh's spring training had made me into a sex fiend. We'd gone from doing it three or four times a week to getting off several times a day—at least I did anyway. We always warmed up with me doing toning exercises on his cock until I climaxed. Sometimes I'd be exhausted from the effort, but he always pushed me on to a second challenge and sometimes even a third. He'd already painted my skin from forehead to toe with his semen. He'd taken me in dozens of new positions, including on every piece of furniture and countertop in the apartment and in the shower. He even pushed me up against the wall in the entryway with the door left open just a crack so that a passerby might catch us—which made me come extra fast and hard.

You might think a woman would get tired of so much sex, but my appetite and stamina were, on the contrary, increasing to meet his demands. Now I felt deprived if I had fewer than three orgasms a day. No doubt about it, no other man I'd known could rival Josh for determination and ingenuity in—and out—of the bedroom.

It was only 2:45, but I was desperate for relief. I grabbed my handbag and hurried down the hall, my gaze focused straight ahead to prevent any colleague from hailing me for a friendly chat.

I purposely headed for the ladies' room at the far end of the hall and dashed inside, heaving a sigh of relief to find it empty. I slipped into the handicapped stall—there were no handicapped employees in my company as far as I knew—and hung my bag over the hook. My new purse was roomy enough to accommodate my dildo and other "exercise" equipment Josh deemed necessary.

Hands trembling, I unzipped my slacks and pushed them midway down my thighs, my damp panties nested inside. I extracted the dildo from its carrying case, a large, quilted makeup bag, and pulled a condom from the inside pouch. I'd discovered the hard way the challenge of washing the thing off afterward in public—best to stuff the condom in the sanitary napkin receptacle and do a proper job at home.

Fortunately, I'd been able to find the perfect six-incher, thick in girth with a ball sac base, at my local woman-friendly sex shop. I'd chosen the "caramel" over "vanilla" because it matched Josh's olive skin. I always felt especially naughty when I rolled the condom over the glans of the fake cock, as if I were cheating on him with another man. When I confessed this to Josh, he teased me that at least I was having safe sex with his second-in-command.

We'd hired a highly able assistant, if I do say so myself.

I positioned the head of the dildo at my entrance and eased it inside, sighing at the satisfying pressure. I was getting addicted to this feeling of fullness, to the implacable resistance as I squeezed my muscles around the shaft. I gave my clit a few flicks and pushed the tool in deeper.

Then I remembered I was supposed to take a picture. I

fumbled in the outside pocket of my purse for the cell phone, one hand holding the dildo firmly inside of me. I switched to camera mode and held the phone, lens side facing me, at groin level. The photo was a little fuzzy, but the obscene content was clear enough: two naked thighs, a hint of pink slit beneath a neatly trimmed bush, the base of the brown cock protruding from my hole, a manicured female hand gripping the balls with assurance. I scrolled down to "send as an email" and typed in the first character of Josh's address. Of course he popped up immediately—he always did—and I pressed send, stifling my laughter.

But soon enough I was lost in lust again. My jaw slack, my eyelids heavy, I pushed the dildo rhythmically in and out with one hand while diddling my clit with the other.

"This is you, Josh. I'm fucking your cock now, and I'm going to come around it," I whispered, just as he'd instructed.

My muscles were so accustomed to the drill that I could usually come with a few minutes of squeezing and a lot of fantasizing. I thought about Josh slapping my ass when I didn't massage his cock hard enough, sending my pussy into helpless spasms of delight. And about how he'd marked every part of me with his hot mouth, his expert hands, his creamy jiz, and his cocks, one flesh, one silicone. I really did belong to him body, mind, and soul, yet at the same time I felt more in control of my desire, more *me*, than ever before.

My cell phone beeped again. I was right on the verge, but I paused to check the message.

"Cum for me."

And model rookie that I was, I did exactly as he said.

Week Five

It was the last Saturday in March, and Coach had me in

bed on my hands and knees, my buttocks thrust out, my forehead pressed into the pillow. I wore nothing, except for a sassy
orange 2010 World Series MVP Edgar Renteria T-shirt, which,
nonetheless, was hiked up to expose my breasts.

"Are you a winner, Erin? Are you willing to go all the way?"

"Yes, Coach," I breathed, wiggling my rear involuntarily.
Josh hadn't yet laid a hand on me, but I already wanted it bad.

"This week we have one final area to master—your ass. And
what a magnificent example of a female posterior it is. I could
just stare at it all day long."

I whimpered. I hoped to hell he'd do more than stare.

"Of course, first we must determine what needs to be accom-
plished. Has anyone ever touched you back there besides me?"

"A little."

"Explain."

"A couple of guys, they put a finger in. But it didn't feel that
good. I like the way you just tease the outside better."

"Well, we'll have to send those 'inept penetration with a
finger' guys down to the minors. Did anyone, including yourself, ever insert another object? A dildo, a butt plug, a tampon?
Or, perchance, one of your favorite zucchini?"

"No, jeez, that's really pervy," I blurted out.

Josh gave me a quick slap on my buttock. I yelped, but more
in pleasure than pain. The sudden smack reverberated through
my body like a hot, undulating wave.

"Your physical conditioning is progressing nicely, but your
attitude still needs work. Anal pleasure, even involving our
good friend, the zucchini, is as much a beautiful expression of
eros as making love in the traditional way."

"Yes, sir," I replied meekly, although I still thought ass play
was wicked—and incredibly hot.

"Did anyone ever fuck you there?"

I hesitated.

"Come on, out with it."

"Once. My college boyfriend, Matt, he just nagged me until I said yes. He used Vaseline, and it was messy and hurt." I grimaced into the pillow at the memory.

"Sorry to hear that. I definitely have a few ideas about how to reeducate your poor little back hole." Josh's voice was suddenly gentle. And so was the touch of his finger as he circled my anus lightly. The sphincter contracted gratefully. I felt the sensation in my chest, too, a warmth that seemed surprisingly pure.

"Last question. Has anyone licked you back there?"

"Never," I sputtered.

"Have you ever licked a man's ass yourself?"

I choked out an "Um, no."

"Well," Josh said, "we have a lot of ground to cover this week. We'll start slow, though. Your ass needs some serious loving and appreciation. So this morning I'll rim you and give an introductory demonstration of proper finger techniques."

"Ah," was all I could say. My belly was on fire, and my ass was blushing as red as my face. Josh was going to put his lips to me back there? His tongue even? Then I really would belong to him, every last naughty bit of me.

"Do your squeezes, Erin, but focus on the muscles in your anus. They need to be strong, too."

"Yes, Coach," I mumbled into the pillow. Josh's program had made me into quite the sexual athlete, and I had no doubt I could climax however and whenever he commanded.

As I clenched and released, a finger began to stroke my valley delicately. In spite of the beguiling stimulation, I did my best to concentrate on my repetitions. But Josh circled the rim, round and round, until I fell forward on the mattress in a quivering heap of delight. Then he drew back.

And slapped me right on the hole.

"Oh, fuck. Oh, fucking fuck," I groaned.

"Hey, are you okay?" Josh was suddenly all concern.

"Yes, yes. Do that again."

Chuckling softly, he spanked me half a dozen times there, methodically, striking the perfect balance between pleasure and pain.

"Push out now," he said. I had one last pang of shyness—how could I ever do something so *bad?*—but then again I wanted to give myself totally to him. Then he would indeed have penetrated me everywhere: my cunt, my mouth, my fantasies—and now my most forbidden place.

The next sensation was an exquisite warmth and wetness. He really was licking me. Was there anything as nasty as this? Yet, as he soothed me with soft little laps of his tongue, the whole lower half of my body, from waist to knees, melted and floated right off the bed. I'd never felt anything like it before.

I was still flying when he pulled away once more.

"Keep squeezing, Erin. I want you to come with my finger up your ass. Are you turned on enough to do it?"

"I am, oh god, I'm so turned on."

"Then repeat after me—this is a beautiful act of love."

"*This is*...wait, you're kidding, right?"

"I won't touch you again until you say the words."

A harsh but effective coaching strategy. And so I began to babble.

This is a beautiful act of love, a beautiful act, a beautiful...

Instead of a tongue, though, my next visitor was a wetted finger that caressed the ring of muscle several times as if to reassure it, then wiggled its way carefully into the opening.

A beautiful act of love...

The finger rested there patiently as if to say, "Let's get to know each other and be friends." I squeezed it hungrily, for my body now knew the magic of his presence. The man I loved was inside of me, intent only on my satisfaction. Another finger slipped forward to find my clit. My thighs began to shake.

"That's a good girl. Milk me. Make my finger a tool of your pleasure. And say the words, Erin. Say the words until you come."

It's a beautiful...act...of...love, oh, god.

I'd never had an orgasm quite like it. A swirling ball of heat gathered at the base of my spine, then rolled up through my pussy, my womb, my torso, exploding in a throat-tearing scream.

Josh just held me for a long time afterward.

"How was that, baby?" he asked, stroking my hair.

What else could I answer?

Beautiful.

Opening Day

The first day of April started off as usual, except for a few clever April Fool's jokes sent out by the HR Department in a fake memo. After work, Josh and I planned to order takeout and watch the Giants–Dodgers game on TV. With spring training now officially over, I expected our personal sessions would taper off, but I hoped we'd still find a way to stay in shape during the regular season.

Yet when Josh got home from work, there was an unusual glow of excitement about him, as if he still had a sexy plan in store for me.

My pussy was already juicing up at the thought.

He held out a small box from my favorite chocolate store. "This is to celebrate the end of training."

Okay, I was a greedy bitch and a total pervert, but my heart sank. A chocolate cock filled with buttercream would have been fitting, perhaps, but after all the wild things we'd done together, a tiny box of truffles was an underwhelming finale, to say the least.

"Let's go cuddle on the sofa," Josh said. He looked a little nervous now. Had he noticed my disappointment?

But by the time he slipped his warm arm around me and pulled me close, I was already feeling better.

"So what did you think of spring training?"

"I'm going to miss it," I answered truthfully.

"It took all I had just to keep one step ahead of you."

"Really? Well, I learned quite a lot, Coach."

"I learned some things, too, and I just wanted to say..." Josh faltered.

I looked at him expectantly, but his eyes darted away.

He cleared his throat and took my hand. "Remember when I said that when we were finished, no other hands, lips, or cock would ever satisfy you again?"

"I remember."

"Well, my ego's not really that big, although on some level I hoped it would be true."

I patted his crotch. "I like your big ego."

He laughed. "Be serious now. I wanted to say that I realized something myself in the past few weeks. The truth is...no other woman could ever satisfy me the way you do."

Now I looked away. I didn't want my coach to catch me crying. Because that was, without a doubt, the sweetest thing any man had ever said to me.

"Have a chocolate," he said, pushing the box toward me.

"Before dinner?"

He shook the box teasingly. It rattled.

Curious, I took it and pulled open the ribbon.

And what should I find inside but three chocolate truffles and a diamond ring.

I had to admit that was one hell of a season opener.

Of course I said I'd marry him then and there. With this kind of chemistry, we had a team that would win it all.

A PREFERENCE
FOR DEFERENCE

Allison Wonderland

I'm in a bind. Not *that* kind of bind. I should be so lucky. It's more like the bind you find yourself in when the love of your life wants you to do something she knows you don't want to do, and you know you can't say no to her because, well, you just can't say no to her. God, am I whipped. Not *that* kind of whipped. I should be...

So my partner Lisa wants me to join her women's bible study group. Now, I enjoy the company of women just as much as the next person, but sanctity just isn't my scene. Lisa's big on it, though, and if she likes it, I guess it can't be all that bad. Besides, maybe the couple that prays together stays together? I've been involved with Lisa for seven heavenly months, and if my secular days are numbered because of Lisa's affinity for divinity, then so be it.

That being said, there's no reason I can't give her a hard time about it. "What kind of right-wing wingding are you schlepping me to?" I grouse, pulling up my pantyhose.

Lisa rolls her eyes and swishes her cinnamon-flavored mouthwash between her cheeks. How does she do that? I can't even pat my head and rub my stomach in sync. "Knock it off, Nancy," she scolds, placing the bottle back on the counter, so that hers is touching mine.

My fingers wrap around the canary-colored handle of Lisa's hairbrush. "Do you realize that it's 8:30 in the morning?" I demand, maneuvering the bristles through Lisa's wavy tresses. "And it's Saturday, for christ's sake. Who in their right mind is awake at such an ungodly hour?"

"Someone's up bright and surly," Lisa quips. Her gaze drifts to the bed, where, only fifteen minutes earlier, we were a snarl of languid limbs and sex-scented serenity. I tuck my chin into her shoulder, settle my head against hers.

"I love you," she says.

"You should."

"You'll thank me later."

"I'll spank you later."

"Fine," she says, and for a second, I think she sounds more cheerful than fearful. Yeah, right. Lisa, she's...well, let's just say that her idea of kinky is making love with the lights on.

On the other hand...she is suspiciously submissive. I know the bible is all in favor of discipline and obedience, but that doesn't mean... Actually, now that I think about it, I wonder if that does mean...I mean, maybe it's possible, I guess, that she...

Nah, forget it. There is no way on God's green earth that Lisa would ever go for any of that rough stuff.

Lisa is bound and determined to make me pay attention. I am paying attention—to her. Lisa's got a body like Jane Russell but dresses like Jane Addams. Except today. It could be my imagination, but I'm almost positive there's something different about her appearance today. Her blouse seems less bulky and less buttoned. Her skirt seems less long and less loose.

I study the outline of her backside. It's a well-rounded rump, the kind that's just cruising for a bruising.

Lisa leans into me. "Why, may I ask, are you so fixated on my fanny?" she demands, the spicy scent of her breath complementing the playful pitch of her voice.

My gaze shifts to the bible sinking into my lap. I'm sure my eyes are as black as its leather binding. God, please let this be over soon.

As if in answer to my prayers, the group leader initiates the closing communion. I like this part. It means I get to hold Lisa's hand openly.

Afterward, Lisa makes me socialize and help eat the donuts that someone brought, none of which have sprinkles.

How much longer are we going to be here? I mean, come on—there's got to be a limit on the number of impure thoughts a person can think inside a house of worship before they get excommunicated.

"Nancy and I will clean up today," Lisa volunteers. Jesus christ, what the hell is she doing?

The fellowship hall clears out, until we're left in the company of bibles and burgundy chairs and acorn-colored tables.

"Did you enjoy that?" Lisa inquires, closing the door. A quiet *click* follows close behind.

"Yes, particularly the story of Sodom and Gomorrah. Who knew it had nothing to do with homosexuality?"

"Yearning *and* learning? My goodness. And you thought you were lousy at multi-tasking."

We lock lips, bump hips.

"Aren't you going to thank me properly?" she pouts.

"I just did."

"I'll rephrase," she says, daintily pinching her skirt between her thumb and index finger. "Aren't you going to spank me properly?"

Lisa flips a chair around, presses it up against a table. She climbs onto the cushion, her knees carving divots into the seat.

My lips leap into a smile. I pitch her skirt up, shove the hem inside the waistband. Her panties are plain, simple, virgin-white. "Is God going to smite you?"

"No," Lisa assures me. "You are."

"So, essentially, I'll be doing God's work?"

Lisa nods, propelling her bottom into my palm as she submits to me, bound by lust and trust. That's all the encouragement I need. I rub her rump, massaging the flesh, tracing halos on her skin with my fingertips.

I study the cheeky curves of her backside. "I have a feeling this is going to hurt me more than it's going to hurt you," I murmur, just before my hand *whomps* her posterior.

Lisa giggles. She steeples her fingers, presses her palms together.

"Lord, have mercy?" I venture, wondering how long it will take to get that Dixie Cups ditty, "Chapel of Love," out of my head.

"No, it's so I don't...you know. So I won't be tempted to touch...myself."

It's then that I notice the aroma. The spanking has barely started, and already I can smell her arousal. It's a succulent scent—cranberries mingled with mandarin oranges.

My palm strikes again. Lisa bounces up and down on her chair. "Easy there, Tigger. I can't hit a moving target."

She stills.

My hand *thumps* her rump.

"My knees hurt," she says.

The poor, sore thing. I just assumed she would suffer in silence. "That's what happens when you pray and play in the same position." I swoop down like a bird of prey. "You get a—"

"Holy fuck!"

Did Lisa just curse? Funny, I figured the only way she would ever swear is in a court of law.

Countless swats, strikes, and smacks later, Lisa is sufficiently smote. I peer inside her undies and study her battered, Barbie-pink backside. My palm is identical in shade. Who knew pleasure could be such a pain?

Speaking of pain... "I'm pretty sure the bible mentions something about doing to others what you would have them do to you."

Lisa climbs carefully off the chair. She yanks her skirt out of the waistband, lets it drop down to her calves. "The bible also says to be patient in affliction."

"Fine," I say, and for a second, I think I sound more fearful than cheerful. Yeah, right.

Lisa licks her lips, rubbing her hands together like Snidely Whiplash.

Yeah. Right.

"Have a seat," she says solicitously, gesturing to the chair.

My legs shudder. Lisa always did make me weak in the knees. I clamber onto the cushion.

"Nancy, dear?" She smiles at me, like an angel of mercy. "You haven't got a prayer."

THE HEART OF CHAOS

Rachel Kramer Bussel

O n the surface, my husband Skip and I might seem unconventional. In a sense, we are, because we don't work
corporate jobs; I'm an artist, the kind who works with paint
and performance, and he's a chef, one I consider to be a food
artist. Yet if one of us is more by the books, it's Skip. Whereas
I consider art my chance to jump into the heart of chaos, to
surrender to the part of me that is wild and wanton and doesn't
play by the rules, he thinks of cooking as something more akin
to a science, perhaps a form of math, full of rules and precision
that, he says, lead to masterpieces.

Most of the time, I agree to disagree, because when we
come together, I win. What I mean by that is chaos wins; he
surrenders his analytical self, unwrapping the layers of over-
thinking to unlock the perfect masochist. In our years together,
I've beaten him, whipped him, gagged him, bound him, pierced
him, and even branded him, once, at his behest. I consider
kink to be a form of chaos too, a place where we go forward

without knowing the next step, where there is no right answer, only multiple paths each leading to its own kind of bliss, like an erotic Choose Your Own Adventure where every ending is a happy one.

I like that we don't necessarily think the same way when we approach our work; otherwise, life would be boring. When I step into my studio, I have only the vaguest idea about what I plan to create, whereas Skip has recipes, road maps, a mental, if not a physical, image of what he wants to concoct for his customers. Recently, though, our worlds collided, and he had to step into mine, to surrender to the chaos, give up any pretense of rationality.

"My show, my show..." was all I could mutter as I sank to the floor of my studio, ready to cry. The canvases themselves were hung, the gallery ready, the poster in the window touting the performance I'd been practicing with my model, Claude, for weeks. It was a tricky, complicated work that involved covering him in Cling Wrap, including his face, with only a mouth hole so he could breathe, then using him as my canvas, layering candle wax everywhere. In the end, I'd rip it off, and he'd put out a flame with his tongue. It this case, my chaos was carefully choreographed; I couldn't just wing something like that, and I wanted people to make the connection among the struggle Claude had to endure, the sense of immobility and surrender, and the art on the walls. Sometimes I felt just as immobile as if I were bound tight all over, not in a sexual sense, but in every other way. Claude got that...but he'd also gotten a very high fever, and there was no way I would've let him go through with it, even if his doctor had okayed it. That left only one choice: Skip.

"Honey, what's wrong? What can I do?" he asked as I rocked myself back and forth on the floor, a plan forming.

"I need you," I said, staring right into his startlingly clear blue eyes, ones that look like that ripest of blueberries. "Claude had to cancel for tonight. He's sick. I need you to take his place."

My husband is one of the palest people I've ever met, but I saw his face go even whiter. "I'll do anything for you, Molly, but not that. I couldn't. It'd be humiliating."

I stood up and walked toward him. "That's exactly the point," I said as I reached for his cock beneath his jeans. "Well, not the only point, but one of them. It's about surrendering to the unknown, letting go. You're telling me you don't want to be tied up, unable to move at all, barely able to breathe?" I'd taken his dick out and started stroking its hard, smooth length.

"What I feel right here in the privacy of your studio is one thing. You know public play is a limit for me, baby." His voice took on a whine as I ran my thumb around the wet tip.

"I'd normally never ask you to disrespect your limit, but this is an emergency. I'm not going to order you to do it, because you're your own person, but I'd be extremely grateful if you'd do this for me this one time. And I also have a feeling you just might like it, if you let yourself go with it."

I stop myself from saying more, even though my natural inclination is always to say more, to go past the point of reason, to fill the empty space with words, as if they will somehow magically create actions. But here words are not my master, and neither, really, is Skip. I must wait and let him think and decide if it's worth it and know that if he declines, I will be okay. I cannot let my opening's entire promise rest on my husband's shoulders.

He looks up at me and says, "Okay, I'll do it, but you know how much this is a sacrifice for me. I'm nervous."

Skip never tells me he's nervous; even when I hear him drawing in breath after breath when I spank or whip him, it's not nerves he's displaying. Those breaths are giving him extra stamina, and he gains strength through submission. But for him that is what we do at home, in private; those are our sacred, beautiful, kinky rituals, ones that are all the more special because they are not for public consumption. He likes that he's known for being unconventional with his work, but when it comes to sex, that just doesn't come up. Someone might say his latest culinary masterpiece is "orgasmic," but they don't mean it literally. I've even seen him blush when someone made that connection too strongly; he doesn't see food the way I do, the mouth connecting to parts much lower.

I know him and love him too much to have asked him to do this if I had any other options, but the more I think about it, the more I realize it might be good for us, to take all the extremes we play with at home and bring them into the world. Of course, it's not going to be a scene in the traditional sense; we can't go quite as far, and it's not about us, really, but our audience. Still, even though I'd never fuck Claude and betray my marriage, I must admit there was a part of me that was looking forward to degrading him, to watching him squirm and struggle, to pushing him beyond his usual limits. That is where I get off on the process; just as I want people to walk away from my art feeling differently than they did walking into a gallery, I want kink to change me and Skip, or whoever I might play with. We are pretty faithful to one another, but once in a while, maybe once a year, we might find ourselves intrigued by someone else and go off and have a romp.

"Okay, well, I have to be there at 6:00 to set up; you can get there at 7:30, and the performance is at 8:00. You've heard me going over the details with Claude so you know what it's going to entail. Mummification, hot wax, and a candle. You can practice that part on your own if you want." I say the words in such a businesslike way, so the opposite of what I feel about them. My heart pounds as I look at my husband's face, watch him try to stay calm, even though I can practically feel his nerves leaping across the few feet that separate us.

"Molly...I don't want this to come between us. This is your work, and I respect that, but we are more than that, right?"

I move closer and pull him in for a hug. "We are always more than that, baby. Always. I love that you're doing this for me, but I'd love you whether you did it or not. Now please pamper yourself today; no chores, do whatever you feel like for the next few hours."

I have to get away from him, so I don't start to feel sorry for him. I lay out my outfit for tonight and gather all the things I'll need; the supplies for the scene are already at the gallery. The owner, Daniel, calls me a few times with last-minute questions, and before I know it there is a crowd lined up outside, and we are getting everything ready. I want these strangers to walk in and see my husband, naked, covered in clear Cling Wrap. I want them to sense what he is feeling, sense what he is offering me, and by extension, them. I want them to go to the heart of chaos with me, live.

Skip's eyes are big as I start to wind the sheer wrap around his ankles, tight enough so he can't move. It's when I get to his cock that I have to smile; despite what I know are true nerves, he's hard, his impressive cock so erect I know that anyone who sees it will be jealous—the men of his size, the women (and I'm sure some of the men) of me. "I love you," I whisper in his ear before I cover it with the wrap. In that moment, it's doubly true, triply. I can't focus on the sappy feelings threatening to overtake me because I have a job to do, but seeing him like that, I'm not only excited about what's about to happen, I'm touched. I know that even if it turns him on like nothing else, if it weren't me asking, Skip would never have agreed to this.

I finish securing the wrap and then use a nail to poke a hole in his mouth, inserting a plastic tube so he can breathe. He can move his body a little by rocking back and forth, and that is his signal if things get to be too much. I've also trained two staffers to watch him closely; at the first sign of anything wrong, we cut him out. Most of this crowd, as avant-garde as they may think they are, have never seen anything like this, I'm sure. The red velvet ropes around my husband have just been secured when the crowd starts streaming in.

In what feels like no time, we are at capacity. Cameras are going off nonstop, and I can hear the word *husband* being whispered along with giggles, gasps, and plenty of profanity. People simply don't know what to make of this. Daniel gets up to introduce me, and I smile, my eyes looking all over, hoping we pull this off without a hitch. I'd practiced with Claude so many times but had only told Skip about those sessions, where he'd winced when I'd described pouring hot wax onto Claude's cock. Yes, it was protected by the Cling Wrap, but not entirely.

I knew that the added drama of our last-minute substitution would have the art world abuzz, but right now, I don't care about that. I've worked so hard to make this the perfect night that I don't want anything to mar it. "And now we will have a five-minute live presentation," I hear booming over a loud-speaker, and then the lights are dimmed, the music starts, and I begin "painting" my human canvas, my husband, with wax. I smile at him, genuinely, as I drip purple all along his chest, arms, and back. When the first candle is nearing its end, I blow it out, toss it on the floor, and am handed a white one. I go into the zone, where it isn't about me and Skip, or even me and the audience, but me and the candles, the canvas, using the colors to work together. I have to move quickly, and the urgency spurs me on.

The room is as silent as a packed gallery can be as I coat my husband from head to toe with hot wax. I can hear him breathing through the tube and see his dick straining against its trappings. I can't take the time to get turned on, but I do smile when I get to the last candle and manually smear it all along his chest, taking a moment to pinch his nipples as I do. I'm handed safety scissors, and I cut him free. The lights come up, and then the trickiest part happens. I'm given a long black candle, and Skip kneels before me. I try my best not to tremble as I upend it. One drop of wax falls on his lower lip, and then I'm staring, riveted, as I place the lit candle in his mouth, where he expertly "swallows" it, extinguishing the flame. The room explodes into applause and Skip stands there stiffly until I tap his arm and tell him he can go change.

The rest of the night flies by, and all the pieces but two wind up with red dots next to them. Skip sticks around, even though I know he'd rather be home, and even though he shrinks from the attention, standing just behind me or in a corner most of the night, I know we've reached some crucial point in our relationship, some space where the chaos of playing in public has permeated our private world.

Finally, the last guest leaves, and he lifts me up in his arms. "I can't believe we did that," he says, and I grab him for a kiss, letting my hand wander down to his ass.

"I can't believe you let me," I say.

"I'd do anything for you," he tells me, his voice shaking with passion.

Just then I know exactly what I want to give him. "You can have me. I mean, do whatever you want to me." Yes, usually I top him, but we've been together for a long time, and sometimes we mix things up. I like to think the rarity of my subbing to him makes it all the more special, but the truth is, we are complex creatures and follow our moods. Suddenly, I want to show him, viscerally, with my body, how much what he's done meant to me.

"Whatever I want?" he asks, his voice taking on a suspicious hint of mischief.

"Well, within our rules."

"Do you have any more candles?" He knows I ordered several times more than I needed, just in case something went awry, as well as for practice.

"Yes."

"Then take off your clothes and get on the tarp."

"Here? Now?" I ask.

"Why wait?" The grin he gives me is pure evil. "Don't tell me it's okay for all the people who work here to have seen me totally nude but not okay for you."

I can't argue with him, and besides, this isn't about anyone but the two of us. "Give me five minutes," I say.

"You're on," he smirks. I tell Daniel what I want to do, and he agrees to leave me in charge.

"You were amazing tonight, Molly. You're a star." I hug him, but just then, the art world, even in the middle of this gallery, seems far away. The only place I want to be is right here, ready to accept whatever my husband gives me.

As I undress, I'm a little nervous, almost shy. I've known Skip for more than a decade and been married to him for six years, but suddenly it's like I'm submitting to him for the first time. In a way, maybe I am, because we've both gone to new places tonight, sharing parts of ourselves we might not have ever seen were it not for a quirk of fate.

I'm not scared of the wax, though; that part my nipples

strain toward, my legs spread for, as he stands over me. I try not to laugh as I see him put on his dom face, and I can tell he's struggling not to ask me exactly how this works. I know for a fact he's never used hot wax like this because we've talked about it; you learn a lot about someone by playing with them, fucking them, loving them for all these years.

But just when I make to laugh, he grabs my wrist and pins it to the floor. There's no laughter in his eyes. He doesn't want to hurt me, but to connect with me in the deepest way we know how, in the give-and-take of pain and pleasure. "Quiet, Molly," he says, and I am, the laughter morphing into something else entirely.

When he coats me with the wax, he does not use theatrical flourishes. He does it for maximum impact, maximum sensation, maximum pain, even though I'm twisted enough to like it...even when he pours red wax directly onto my shaved pussy. I flinch, I even scream a few times, but the hotter it gets, the more I like it. I alternate between keeping my eyes closed and watching the wax land directly on my skin until finally I'm just looking at Skip, my Skip. When he grabs two lit candles and pours the wax directly onto my nipples, smiling down at me, trying to break me, I smile up at him before I give in to the pain. I scream and yet I don't try to back away, don't even think about using my safe word. I just go there with him, into the chaos, into the fire, until I'm coated in wax, everywhere but my face.

When he's done, he grabs me and pulls me toward his cock, and I take him all the way down. I feel the tip land against the back of my throat, and I let him shove himself into me again and again. I let myself cry even as the most blissful sensations wash over me in waves. He pulls out after a few minutes, plants himself between my legs, and skewers me with his cock. "I'd do anything for you, anything," he says almost viciously as his hardness drills inside me.

"I know you would. I would too." And then he takes me exactly where he wants me, with him, to somewhere magical. Naked on a tarp in the middle of an art gallery, covered in wax, with my husband on top of me, I can't think of anywhere I'd rather be.

UNDER
THE CLOCK

Justine Elyot

I wait, as instructed, until the long hand points directly at the six and the short hovers a few degrees to its right. This is my signal to step out from the ticket barrier and cross the concourse, its marble-effect flooring scarred by years of stilettos and cigarette butts, pirouetting lovers and blood-pressured businesspeople. I try to blend in, but attention is not easily deflected when one is wearing a second skin of black latex, fishnets, and four-inch-heeled ankle boots. The leash that dangles from my collar, swinging between my rubber-cased breasts, doesn't help either.

Concentrating on walking in a straight line without wobbling, I stare determinedly through the nudges and whistles until I am in my place. Under the clock.

From my vantage point, shoulders back, eyes front, hands clasped behind back, I let the rush hour flow around me, a blizzard of briefcases and flapping ties, instructions barked into mobile phones, wafts of scents by Giorgio Armani and Jo

Malone among the sweat and diesel fumes. How long will he make me wait?

This is where we first met. It wasn't rush hour then, it was midmorning on a weekday, so the people passing weren't in such a hurry—for the most part shoppers and tourists. I had been told to wait under the clock. I wasn't dressed to draw attention that day, but I knew—and he knew—that underneath the demure polka-dot dress I was wearing some of Agent Provocateur's flimsiest, filthiest merchandise.

I clamped my thighs together, rubbing the suspenders so that the snaps pressed into my skin. Was this a mistake? What would happen? Would he even turn up?

I may be a little late. Don't go. Wait under the clock for me.

That had been his last text message, a quarter of an hour before my train had pulled into the station. I had stood there for half an hour, huffing and clicking my tongue, looking around at all the different shops and cafés that lined the vast space, boredom tempting me into a spot of people-watching. *God, this basque is pinching me.* Beautiful people at the coffee shop, slouchy teenagers at the burger bar, amazing outfits and outlandish piercings—at least he had chosen an interesting place for me to stand doing nothing for all this time. A man at a table outside Costa Coffee folded his newspaper and sat sipping, looking at his watch now and then.

A young man, a tourist, walked up to me and asked me if I knew how to get to Hampton Court Palace.

Don't speak to anyone.

I shrugged, shook my head.

He looked as if he wanted to say something else and hung around for a moment, so I turned my face away. He half-laughed, embarrassed, and trudged off.

I thought about leaving. The man from Costa Coffee stood up and I realized that it was him, just clean shaven instead of the bearded sophisticate in the photograph.

My legs almost gave way beneath me, and I leaned back against the pillar for support, watching him approach, unsure of what to do with my facial features.

"You made me wait," I accused. "You were there all along."

"I wanted to see if you would wait. You did."

He held out a hand.

"Let's go."

"I'm...not into mind games." The words stumbled. I wanted to be assertive, but his presence in my real physical space overwhelmed me too much.

"Mind games? That wasn't a mind game. That was a test. You passed. Even if you'd failed, it wouldn't have mattered. I just wanted to know what you would do. Besides, it's always interesting to watch people who don't know you're there."

His words come back to me now, and the nape of my neck prickles. I wonder if he is watching me from some hidden spot. He is not at Costa Coffee; in his place a harassed woman with a toddler, cake crumbs everywhere. If I search among and between the endless flood of commuters, they will think I'm looking at them, and look back. I work on an impenetrable glaze for my eyes and concentrate on the feeling of erotic compression the rubber gives me, of being tightly packaged, wrapped up with a dog-leash bow on top. Every curve and bump is cartoonishly emphasized, and of course I can't wear anything underneath. The stale station air flows up my micro-miniskirt and over my bare pussy. It's damp. I can feel sticky dew at the tops of my thighs, something to do with all the eyes on me, every man in the station looking sideways and filing the sight away for leisurely contemplation on the train home. I know what they're thinking. I'm dressed to be fucked. I'm collared and owned. If only I was theirs…could I be theirs?

I swallow and clench my pelvic floor, not wanting to add the scent of my arousal to the hurly-burly of mingling aromas. I can't see the clock, but ten minutes must have passed by now. Twenty to six. How much longer?

I didn't know what to expect on that first day. Would he whisk me straightaway to some hotel, undress me and use me in every way possible? No. He took me to an exhibition at the National Gallery, then a lunchtime concert at St. Martin in the Fields. I was touched. I sensed, beneath the suavity and sureness, a vulnerability. It was important to him that I recognized his humanity as well as his sexuality. *I might want to hurt you and whip you and fuck your arse, but look, I love Haydn and Millais. I'm more than that man who makes monstrous suggestions to you via IM.*

It wasn't until he had poured tea and filled my plate with petits fours—I'd never seen a petit four before—at the Ritz that the subject of sex reared its ugly, lovely, scary, brutal, sweet, confusing face.

"What are you wearing underneath that pretty dress?"

I stared down at the snow-white linen, thankful for the loud conversation the elderly American women at the next table were enjoying.

"Don't be shy, Liv. I've asked you a direct question. I expect a direct answer."

"The things you said."

"The things I said? Do they have names?"

I couldn't get used to him without the beard. I made my eyes climb up the ridge of his nose, seeking his crinkled brown-green gaze, then lowered them again before he could...what? Read my thoughts?

"Basque," I whispered. "Suspenders. Stockings."

"Anything else?"

"Knickers."

"Describe them."

"Floral. Lacy."

"And...?"

"Not a thong. Boy shorts."

"I prefer that style anyway. I'd like to see them."

"Oh..." I looked around, then looked at the cakes on my plate, wondering if I was about to be whisked off to a room upstairs. Would we be allowed to take the glass of champagne?

"Not here." He laughed. "At least, not today. Finish your tea and let's go."

In Green Park, up against a tree, watching the open-topped tour buses rumble up and down Piccadilly, I lifted my skirt for him.

He made me turn around, giving my bottom a light but resounding smack before allowing me to drop the hem again.

"Are you wet?"

"Yes."

"Liv, do you want to...as the young people say...get a room?"

"Yes."

Ten to six. He isn't in Tie Rack, though he has been known to use their products as bondage accessories. A man in a suit stops dead when he sees me and stares at me with disarming frankness.

He cranes his neck toward the departures board, assessing perhaps whether he has time to stop and gawp before rushing for the suburbs. Then he walks over to me.

I smarten up my posture, standing to attention.

Speak to nobody.

"Are you waiting for someone?"

I nod, avoiding his eye.

"That's some outfit you're wearing. Is it for his benefit? The boyfriend?"

I swallow. This man is standing quite close now. When he picks up the leash and trails it across his palm, I cannot quite hide my flinch.

"Does he walk you around on all fours?"

I shut my eyes for a second or two. When I open them, he is still there. He is good-looking, his voice is gentle, but his words aren't.

"Well? I asked you a question, Liv. Does Reuben walk you around on all fours?"

He laughs again, enchanted, as my mouth drops open. Reuben's words come back to me...*a surprise for your anni-versary...something we've discussed before...something very special....*

"He's waiting for us. Come on."

Is this a trick? A test? Reuben said I was to wait for him, not the other way around. He said I was not to move until he arrived.

I catch the stranger's lustful eye for a moment and shake my head.

"Oh, what a good girl," he coos, stroking me under the chin before trying to curl a finger inside my collar. "All the same, I'll wait here with you." His hand is heavy against my hip, rubbing the latex. He steps up close to me, pressing his pelvis in its tailored trousers into my rubbery stomach and covers my mouth with his. Hot breath surges between my lips as the stranger's kiss gathers steam. His tongue flickers inside me, darting about, finding my hidden recesses. I keep my hands behind my back and submit to it, the reality of my surrender to this unknown man stirring me into a swoon of lust.

He finds my bottom, snug in its rubber case, an emphasized curve that he follows to its end. He grunts into my throat, then breaks the kiss.

"I bet this makes a lovely sound when he spanks you."

He pats it lightly, as if contemplating finding out for himself. My legs dissolve.

"Never mind. Perhaps he'll show me...if you decide that's what you want."

I look up sharply.

Behind his shoulder, I see Reuben.

"You've met Luke, I see."

"She didn't introduce herself," grins the stranger. "I hope I got the right girl."

"You got the right girl." Reuben pulls me close and kisses me passionately while the station loudspeaker echoes around and above the dull roar of the rush hour. "Tell me what you're thinking, Liv. I never know what you're thinking."

This is true. He used to be just as tight knit, but I unpicked his stitches, one by one, and now I can recite him like the alphabet. He has never pulled off the same trick with me.

"I'm thinking how much I love you."

"Now I have a question for you. You can leave here with me, or with Luke, or with both of us. Or, indeed, alone. Which shall it be?"

I unclasp my hands, stretch out my aching arms, one to each man.

I sit between them on the tube, while Luke fidgets with my leash, tugging it sometimes so that my neck inclines toward him.

They escort me off at Piccadilly Circus and cross with me

to the statue of Eros, beneath which they take turns to kiss and fondle me while the European students and teenage runaways look on, enthralled.

After cocktails at the Criterion, we head into Soho, no longer standing out so much. They take me into a seedy hotel and make a meal of booking a room, making sure that the receptionist knows exactly what we are there for.

"You didn't forget the floggers, did you?" Reuben asks languidly of Luke as we are led up creaky stairs to a stifling room.

"Enjoy your stay," says the porter, poker faced.

"Oh, we will." Reuben smiles and hands him a folded banknote.

My anniversary gifts are the red stripes laid across my bottom and thighs, the two sets of DNA imprinted on my cunt and my arsehole, the bite marks on my breasts and neck, the ache in every muscle. Shakily taped recordings of our debauchery will be my memento, along with the rope burns on my wrists and ankles. Perhaps we will put them on KinkTube one day.

Lying between and beneath them in the cigarette-smelling sheets, I contemplate the journey so far. That polka-dotted girl would not have done this, but that polka-dotted girl didn't love him yet, as she does now.

"How long would you have waited?" asks Reuben, yawning. "Under that clock."

Until darkness fell. Until the last train. Until the cleaners swept their wide brooms across the pocked concourse. Until my legs gave way. Until my latex perished. Until my wrists seized up.

"Until you came."

STEPS

Evan Mora

Fifty feet of rope, so soft it could be skin, uncoiling like a sensuous lover. I've had this rope for a very long time; you, I've only had for eight weeks. You're naked and waiting, standing perfectly still. I guess it's time to begin.

One: Take the middle point of the rope and place it around the back of the neck, making sure the top of the loop just touches the small of the back.

I love how strong your neck is. It was one of the first things I noticed about you, that, and the fact that your Adam's apple bobbed when you were nervous, a giveaway that I've come to be intimately acquainted with, though I'm not even sure you're aware of it.

You were trying so hard to be calm and collected that first night, pretending to be something other than what you were, a nervous boy with fantasies.

Your hands reach up out of reflex now, holding the rope in place gently while I begin to fashion your harness.

* * *

Two: Tie an overhand knot, just above the center of the sternum,
and a second several inches lower.

"You understand what the arrangement is to be, Joshua?"
I had asked, face impassive, although inside a hungry curiosity was already awakening, stretching wide and reaching
out, taking in your young lean frame, strong, but not yet overmuscled, your wide shoulders and long legs, and your carefully
disheveled hair. I imagined already peeling back your layers, the
clothes from your body, your ego, your pride, until I reached the
meat of you.

"Yes, Ms. Gray."

"Ma'am."

"Yes Ma'am." You spoke softly and looked down, wheat-
colored lashes fanning out across pale cheeks, hiding beautiful
gold-flecked green eyes.

"Tell me then, please—so we're both certain." I said, closing
the distance between us.

"You need someone to paint your house...." You broke off as
I circled behind you, fingertips trailing down your arm.

"May I touch you, Joshua?"

"Yes, Ma'am. Yes...please." I smiled, but you couldn't see it.
I asked you to continue, while I eased your plaid shirt down and
off, and you did, your voice hesitant at first, and then rushed.

"Um..." You cleared your throat as I circled back 'round,
sliding my palms beneath your T-shirt. "You need someone to
paint your house, and in exchange..."

"In exchange?" Your abdominal muscles were tense beneath
my fingertips, and your skin felt hot and smooth.

"...you'll spank me. I mean you'll discipline me." Your gaze
met mine and then skittered away, a blush rising in your cheeks.

"Is that what you want, Joshua?" I explored your skin, your

ribcage, your chest, circling the flat disc of your nipple. Your breath caught for a moment, and your nipple hardened when I grazed it with a manicured nail.

"Yes, Ma'am." You spoke quietly, almost a whisper, the naked yearning in your voice as sensual as a lover's touch on my skin, and I felt the beginnings of desire.

Three: Continue this line of knots down the center of the chest at equal intervals, past the navel, placing one knot just above the pubic bone, and a final knot resting between the legs, passing the penis and scrotum through.

You began in the bedroom, at my instruction, which was both fitting and a bit of a tease. I'd left a few choice implements on my bedside table, and you eyed them nervously, your Adam's apple working as you swallowed rapidly.

"I want to see your best work, Joshua." I'd said, and you certainly didn't disappoint. When you were finished, the room looked perfect, and in turn, I kept my end of the bargain, taking you over my knee and administering your payment, one blow at a time, until your backside was a hot and even red beneath my hand.

I wish I could tell you how beautiful you'd looked lying on my bed, your lashes spiked with tears, your body quivering in the aftermath of the spanking, your cock hard and achingly erect.

That was where our arrangement ended. When I was going to tell you to leave. Services rendered, payment received.

"Stroke your cock for me, Joshua." I said instead, even though I hadn't intended to.

You wrapped your fist around your cock, and I couldn't look away. I loved watching the play of emotions across your face; the way the muscle in your jaw tensed; the way your eyes never,

ever left mine. I loved the juxtaposition of your strength and vulnerability, and the way your lips parted around the word *please*.

I kissed you.

I leaned over and breathed in the heady smell of your sweat and arousal and cologne and I kissed you; swept my tongue into the heat of your mouth and slipped my hand beneath yours on your cock. You came for me, and I swallowed the sound with my mouth.

Four: Draw the rope between the legs, and upward to pass through the loop at the top of the small of the back.

I've been quick and efficient while knotting the front of the harness, but I take my time now, drawing the long length of rope through this loop on your back. The rope transmits sensation, and so even the slight vibration of rope passing over rope echoes in your swelling cock. You moan softly, and I press my lips against the skin between your shoulder blades, where I imagine, if you were an angel, you'd have wings.

"Have you ever been bound, Joshua?"

Three weekends and as many spankings later, you'd painted your way through the master bath, guest room and bath, and were preparing to paint my office. You were naked from the waist up, and I was sitting at my desk, watching the play of muscle beneath your gold-hued skin, admiring your forearms and biceps, your shoulders and chest, the wide, beautiful expanse of your back.

"Yes, Ma'am." You'd smiled at me, a perfect slash of white across your handsome young face. "My girlfriend in college used to tie me to the bed when we had sex."

We hadn't had sex yet. I'd watched you come in the aftermath of each spanking, either by my hand or your own, and I'd come too, later though, after you'd gone home. The hesitation was mine; I think even then I'd worried about the shy adoration in your eyes. You were so young, nearly fourteen years junior to my thirty-nine, and young enough still to dream dreams of forever and ever when I didn't believe anymore.

Still though, you were under my skin whether I admitted it or not, and any reservations I had were inexorably overshadowed by desire.

"Belts and scarves tied to the bed frame?" You nodded. "How would you like to try something different?"

Japanese rope bondage, I'd explained as you stripped off your jeans and boxers, had a much greater aesthetic appeal and could be used either to immobilize or simply to decorate.

"For example," I'd said, fashioning a simple diamond-weave body harness from your neck to your groin, "I could use this harness as a base for more elaborate bondage, but it's also comfortable enough to be worn for an extended period of time."

You had a slightly glazed look in your eyes and a fair-sized erection by the time I'd finished, and I tweaked your nipple to get your attention.

"Huh?" You returned to me.

"Put your jeans back on, Joshua; you've got a room to paint."

"But—" A pained look crossed your face, but a stern look and a raised eyebrow stopped your words before they could escape.

"Yes Ma'am," you said. It was a bit sulky, but I let it pass and settled back into my desk chair to work. Well...to work, and to watch you.

And when you'd finished the room to my satisfaction, a task made difficult, I know, by the slight but constant shifting and pulling of the harness against your skin, you weren't the only one in a heightened state of arousal.

I took your hand and led you to my bedroom, pressed you down into the softness of my bed. I stripped off your jeans, caressing your cock and balls briefly before producing four additional lengths of rope. I tied each length into a simple restraint, securing first your wrists and then your ankles to the bed so that you lay spread-eagled before me.

Already your eyes were half-closed, your hips restless against the bed. I ran my nails experimentally along the sensitive skin of your inner thigh, hard enough to mark without breaking skin. Your sharp intake of breath was followed by a moan, a tensing of muscle beneath skin. I marked your other thigh with similar lines, watched as you tried to strain closer to my touch. I circled the base of your cock with one hand, cupping your sac gently with the other. I stroked you like that, teasing you, until I could feel drops of moisture beading at the tip of your cock and a sheen of perspiration covered your chest.

I tightened my grip on your cock then, squeezing your shaft while I twisted your balls, pulling them down so that a hoarse cry was torn from your lips. Your body arched off the mattress, all of your muscles corded tightly, your head tipped back, eyes shut against the pain. But even so, even then, your cock never flagged, seemed instead to grow harder in my hand.

This was what I loved. Watching how beautifully you suffered. For me. We had barely delved beneath the surface, you and I, and yet I knew already that your capacity for suffering was great; greater even, than you knew. I wanted to hurt you in ways that I knew would bring you to a point you didn't think you could tolerate, and then to hurt you enough to push you blindingly, brilliantly beyond. I wanted to take you into a space of pure sensation, and when it was over, I wanted to hold you on the other side, kiss your forehead, and whisper that everything would be alright.

But we weren't there yet, and I didn't know if we'd ever get there. All I knew with certainty at that moment was that I wanted you more than I'd wanted anything in a very long time. And so I removed my clothes and lay on the bed beside you, bracing my weight on my elbow and sliding my thigh over yours. My breasts pressed against your chest and harness, my sex pressed against your hip, I kissed you; pinched and teased the rock hard pebbles that were your nipples; ground my arousal into your skin.

"I want you inside me, Joshua," I whispered against your lips.

"Yes Ma'am, yes please." You shivered beneath me.

I retrieved a foil packet from the bedside table, tore it open with teeth and one hand. I stroked your erection, then rolled on the tight sheath, and then straddled your hips, letting the head of your cock tease my opening without quite pressing inside.

"Please…," you said, and I lowered myself onto you, taking you slowly, deeply inside.

I took hold of your harness, gripping the rope tightly where it came together in a V just above the knot in the center of your sternum, using it to brace myself as I rode you, clenching my muscles around you, milking your cock, slowly, then with greater urgency until we were both falling over the edge and I collapsed against your chest.

When I'd recovered, I'd unfastened your wrists and ankles, and we'd lain together until the room was dark, your head resting against my heart.

"Thank you Ma'am…."

"Juliet," I said. "For now, just call me Juliet."

Five: Split the lines, drawing each beneath an arm and around to the front of the body. Bring the rope underneath the first knot and in between the two lines, pulling it through and cinching

snug, but not tight, then back underneath, the lines just pulled
through, locking the harness in place and holding the tension.

Another weekend to finish the upstairs hallway, and then you
were on to the main floor: living room, kitchen, dining room,
and powder room. A month of weekends remained until you'd
be finished. Until our arrangement would end. That's what I'd
told myself; what I told you.

You'd whispered to me in the dark, when our hearts had
slowed and the air had cooled our heated skin, whispered that
you could be my boy, that you could stay with me. Hadn't I
wanted to finish my basement? You could do that, you'd said.
And what about the exterior of the house? Hadn't I wanted to
repaint it? You could do that too.

But I saw your dreams. Where you'd add a picket fence and
paint it white, and then want a dog, and maybe a swing set. I
was never going to be that person. It didn't matter that you told
me otherwise; said that wasn't what you wanted. Someday, I
knew, you might change your mind. Better to leave things the
way they were.

Still though, you had half of the house left to paint. And
so every Friday night for the next three weeks, you arrived at
my house just after 6:00, and a ritual of sorts was born. You
stripped off your clothes and stood quietly while I drew the rope
around your neck and tied your harness. Then your jeans went
back on, and you'd paint for an hour or two, we'd have dinner,
and then I'd take you upstairs to my bedroom. You didn't go
home those nights anymore—it didn't make sense to go home
when you'd be back again first thing in the morning anyway.
Saturday you'd paint and I'd watch, or you'd paint and I'd work,
depending on my mood.

Saturday night we'd play, and I say play because really,
it wasn't just about spanking you anymore. I had a sizable

collection of toys, and I introduced you to the nuances of each in turn: floggers, paddles, and crops; nipple clamps; anal plugs (you were especially fond of those); and my personal favorite, a rattan cane. Each Saturday night we went a little further, a little deeper. And you opened to each experience completely, with more honesty and humility than I've seen in far more experienced boys. I found you indescribably beautiful.

We didn't get to the cane until the third Saturday night. You were bent over my desk, secured at wrist and ankle. You were making happy sounds, endorphins humming through you, your ass already rosy and hot from my flogger. I began by simply tapping you with the cane—a gentle introduction that produced only a mild sting—but definitely a new sensation after the heavier thud of the flogger.

"Joshua, I'm going to give you three strokes with this cane, okay?"

"Mm-hmm." You sounded dreamy and far away.

"I need you to pay attention, Joshua, because this is going to feel very different than anything we've tried so far."

It was an understatement, to be sure; a hard strike with a cane felt like a knife edge of fire and lightning that blotted out every other thought and sensation, and as the initial blaze faded, an aftershock—still sharp and localized, but with a bit of dull achiness—began to sink in, as though the stripe ran clear to the bone and beyond. I knew this because I didn't believe in using anything I hadn't tried myself, and in my experience, there was nothing that compared to a cane.

"Are you ready?"

"Yes, Ma'am," you said, without any hesitancy at all.

I laid the first stripe across the center of your ass and you screamed, trying instinctively to rear up and away from the pain. You nearly lifted the desk off the ground, but I was right there, stroking your neck, whispering in your ear, telling you how proud I was of you, kissing your cheek and tasting the tears that fell there.

"It's okay, baby," I soothed. "Only two more to go."

"No, I can't, it's too much...."

"Yes you can baby. You're doing so well. You can do this. For me." I stood up.

"Okay, okay, okay..." It was a chant; your eyes squeezed shut, your muscles so tense they could have snapped.

I caressed you, gentle strokes from the small of your back to the tops of your thighs, moving tenderly over the angry red stripe of the cane until I felt you relax. Then quickly, I laid the second stripe just above the first, before you could tense your muscles again. Your scream was raw, like a wounded animal, and your body tried desperately to fold in on itself, make itself smaller.

"Please," you sobbed uncontrollably, "I can't, I can't do this." Your eyes rolled wildly, seeking some kind of escape, but I was there, filling your vision, so that all you could see was me.

"Yes you can, Joshua." I held your chin, stilling your movement.

"No, no more. Please," you pleaded.

"Ssshhh..." I placed a finger across your lips. You were so strong. So beautiful. We had agreed on a safe word before your first spanking, and I was confident I'd hear it if you truly felt you couldn't take any more. I brushed my fingers through the hair that clung damply to your forehead, held your gaze with my own.

"One more." I said, willing you to hold on.

"One more." Your eyes blazed with pain and desperation, but you held my gaze like a drowning man would a lifeline, and I knew that you could finish.

I caressed you like I had before, long, tender strokes across your bruised flesh, and when your muscles began to relax, I laid the last stripe, just below the first.

Your scream filled all the empty space in the house, then subsided into a low, keening wail. I laid down my cane and unfastened your restraints, kissing and stroking you, guiding you down the hall and into bed. You had the glassy, unfocused look of someone who was floating, and I held you and kissed you until you came back to me. And when our kisses became deeper and more sensuous than before, I lay on my back and took you inside me, and somewhere in the darkness, you said, "I love you."

Six: Draw the rope around the back of the body, cross the lines and draw them back to the front, underneath the next knot and in between the lines again, drawing the rope through, cinching and pulling tight. Do this with each knot in turn, creating a diamond pattern along the torso. When the last knot is completed, tie off a square knot at the back of the harness.

And now here we are. The last of our weekends. I finish tying the square knot that completes your harness and step back to admire you. Your body so strong, your cock thick and ready with anticipation, your beautiful eyes, shining with trust, and yes, love—I can't deny that. There are things I want to do to you—with you—ways I want to hurt you that we haven't even touched upon yet, and I know that you'll go there with me, that your trust will never waver. We're a matched pair, you and I, and you need these things as much as I do. You smile at me, a gentle curve of your lips that tells me you know—what I'm thinking; what I'm feeling; that maybe next week we'll start working on the basement—and I think, right now, that I might love you.

BRUSHSTROKES

Kristina Wright

They had been together for six months. Mai Ling dipped her paintbrush in water and glided it across the blank white board in front of her. The water made a dark, swirling stain on the board.

Six months was long enough, she thought, to know whether someone is right. Whether there was a future. She stared at the board, watching the mark she had just made evaporate.

It wasn't that she didn't love him. She did. She dipped the brush once more, applied it to the board, and with a flick of her wrist created her design. Quickly, before it could disappear, she picked up more water on the brush and dragged it over the first mark. The one beneath was already fading as she finished the design on top.

He just wasn't right for her. He was so brash, so outspoken. She was quiet, reserved, cautious. He wasn't. He didn't fit into her life. He wanted her to be more like him, more outgoing. She wanted...she wasn't sure what she wanted. She had, at first, loved his ability to say anything. Especially when they were in bed. She would hide her face behind her hair, her cheeks flushed with embarrassment, but his words warmed her in other places. Made her hot and needy for him, the feel of his body, so dark and muscular and different.

Her hand moved frantically over the board, filling up the space with slash marks.

She sensed his frustration. She knew he wasn't happy with her proper, ladylike ways. He wanted something more. Something she couldn't give. Something she didn't have in her. She stared at the board. It was as blank as when she had started.

She felt Gregory's hands on her shoulders before he spoke.

"What are you doing?"

She shrugged, not turning around. "Painting."

He laughed. "There isn't anything there."

"It's Zen," she said. "It's about living in the moment, working out your frustrations and then starting over with a clean slate."

He kneaded her shoulders gently. "What are you frustrated about?"

He knew. She *knew* he knew. She still couldn't say. She shrugged. "Just...things."

Gregory knelt beside her chair. "Tell me, Mai Ling," he said quietly.

She didn't want to look at him. The painting ritual hadn't given her the peace she needed to make a decision. "It's nothing."

He took her hand. "You have to talk to me. You never tell me what's wrong."

"That's our problem, isn't it?" she asked, shaking off his touch. "We don't know how to talk to each other."

He sat back on his heels, as if surprised at her angry tone. "I've never had a problem talking to you."

"Right. Right. It's my problem," she said, feeling trapped, angry. "I can't talk to you. I can't be like you."

He tried to take her hand again, but she wouldn't let him. He settled for putting his hand on her bare thigh, right below the hem of her skirt. "Mai Ling, I don't want you to be like me. I just want us to be close."

She stared at his hand on her bare leg. The contrast between their skin tones always surprised her. His darkness against her paleness. Even in summer when she would spend so much time at the beach and she was as dark as her brother who worked in landscaping, she was still fair next to Gregory. She usually loved the difference in their skin tones, but now it seemed just one more reminder of how different they were.

"This isn't working, Gregory," she said softly. "You know it, too."

He held her leg tighter, his long fingers curving around her slender thigh. "I don't know that. I don't believe it. Just talk to me, Mai Ling. Talk to me."

She opened her mouth. Closed it. There were no words. She shook her head. "I can't."

They stayed like that, him kneeling beside her, his hand on her thigh, her staring at the blank board in front of her. She willed him to leave, to walk away, to make it easier for her. He stayed. She picked up the paintbrush and dipped it in water. Pressing it to the board, she wrote her name. As it faded, she dipped the brush in the water and wrote his name beneath hers. By the time she wrote the *y* in Gregory, her name was gone and the first letters of his name were fading.

"That's what is happening to us, isn't it? We're fading away." He stood. Finally, he was going to leave.

She didn't know what made her do it, but she wrote on the board, "Don't go."

She wasn't sure if he'd seen it until she felt his hand on her shoulder. "You want me to stay?"

She wrote, "Yes." She thought for a moment, then wrote, "I need you."

"You have to tell me what you need," he said.

She couldn't look at him. Her face was burning. She wrote, "I can't. I don't know how."

He didn't speak. He stroked her hair. It soothed her. Carefully, she wrote, "I don't know how to tell you what I need." She watched the words fade, then wrote, "I'm scared."

"Don't be scared," he said. "Write it."

She thought about it, the words jumbled up in her mind so that she didn't know where to start. "You're so strong," she wrote. "But with me, you're so gentle."

"Gentle is bad?" he asked.

She bit her lip in frustration. Even in writing she couldn't make herself clear. She tossed the paintbrush down on the desk, feeling the hot sting of tears behind her eyelids.

He reached over her, picked up the brush and put it in her hand. "Try again. I'm not going anywhere."

She took the brush from him. She wrote, "You treat me differently. You protect me when I don't need protecting. I want you to stop treating me like I'm going to break."

"Emotionally or physically?"

She didn't hesitate to write, "Both."

"I feel like a big, dumb ox next to you," he said. "You're so graceful and gentle and proper."

She shook her head. "I'm not. You're not," she wrote. "No, no, no."

As each *no* faded, she wrote another. Finally, he laughed. "Okay, I get it. I'm sorry."

She wrote, "I can't say what I need." The words faded, each

brushstroke becoming lighter until it was gone. "But I still *need*."

"What do you need, Mai Ling?" he asked softly, his fingers pulling gently through her hair.

"Harder," she wrote.

He wrapped his fingers in the long strands of her dark hair and pulled. "Like that?"

"Harder," she wrote, in thicker, darker letters.

He pulled until her head was pulled back and he was looking into her eyes. "Like that?" he asked again.

She waited for him to release his grip on her hair, then she nodded slowly.

"What else do you need?"

She held the paintbrush poised above the blank board. "I need you to," she wrote. She couldn't finish it.

"What, Mai Ling?"

She shook her head. She couldn't write it.

"Do you want me to leave you alone?"

She shook her head hard.

"What, then? What do you need?"

She wrote the words again. "I need you to," she wrote, hesitating once more. "To have sex with me." It wasn't right, but it was there.

He didn't speak for a minute, and by the time he did her words were gone. "You want me to make love to you?" He sounded as confused as she felt.

She shook her head quickly. "No," she wrote.

"But you wrote—"

She shook her head again. Carefully, deliberately, she wrote, "Not make love."

"You wrote you need me to have sex with you," he said. "But you don't want me to make love to you."

She nodded slightly. "Not make love, not sex," she wrote. "I need you."

"Mai Ling, you're not making sense."

She waited for the words to fade. Then quickly, before she could lose her nerve, she wrote in broad, heavy strokes, "Fuck me."

She heard his quick intake of breath. She had never used that word until now. "Okay."

She smiled. He sounded shaken. Rattled. The way he made her feel sometimes. It gave her an odd sense of power. "Fuck me," she wrote again. "Hard."

His breathing had quickened, his fingers tightening on her shoulders. "Are you sure?"

She nodded even as she wrote. "Hard. Rough."

He caught her hair up in his hand, dragging his fingers through it so that her scalp tingled. "Hard, rough," he repeated, his voice deepening. Collecting her hair again, he gave it a sharp tug. "Like this?"

Mai Ling gasped. "Oh yes," she said aloud, no need to write her desire on the board. "Please."

He pulled her up by her hair, twisting it so that she turned to face him. She was nearly a foot shorter than him, and he pulled her hair so that she had to look up at him. Neck arched, eyes wide, she stared into a face that was both familiar and unfamiliar.

"Tell me, Mai Ling," he whispered. He studied her, his face set in solemn lines. "I want to hear the words."

She tried to duck her head away from his unrelenting gaze, but he held her hair fast. "I can't," she whispered, even softer than him. "I can't."

Tears pricked her eyes, fear that failing his test meant he would give up. And that would be the end of them. Instead, he nodded.

"You will."

Threat or promise, she wasn't sure. But it made her nipples harden and wetness pool between her legs. "Yes," she responded, almost by accident.

He picked up her paintbrush from the desk and handed it to her. "Show me what you want."

A shiver of anticipation dance along her spine. She could play this game. She could do anything he asked as long as she didn't have to speak.

Dipping the paintbrush in the cup of water, she held it between them, hesitating. Did she have the nerve?

"Show me what you want," he said again, his voice hard, his hand tight in her hair.

With a trembling hand, she lowered the wet tip of the paintbrush to the crotch of his jeans and drew a line along the ridge of his erection. Then she looked up at him.

"You want my dick."

It was a statement, not a question, but she nodded anyway.

"Good girl," he said. "Where do you want my dick?"

Again, she hesitated. The obvious thing to do was to mark her own crotch, leaving a wet mark on the outside of her pants to match the wetness inside her panties. Instead, she dipped the paintbrush in water and held it to her mouth like a lipstick. She painted the water on her lips and then, kitten-quick, she licked the tip of the paint brush.

"Holy hell," Gregory groaned. "I'm going to come in my pants if you do that again."

A surge of feminine power rushed through her, making her feel suddenly, vibrantly sexual. She giggled, then licked the paintbrush again.

Gregory released her hair and dropped his hands to her shoulders. With a gentle pressure, he let her know what it was he wanted. She slipped to her knees in front of him, studying the wet mark on his jeans.

"This is what you want?" he asked, unzipping his pants and releasing his erection. "You're sure?"

She nodded, staring up at him, suddenly shy. She'd never knelt like this in front of him, had never gone down on him in the light of day, even. When it came to sex, she was always unsure of her abilities, no matter how appreciative Gregory might be. Other lovers, the few she'd had, had seemed as content as she with the basics of sex. Something inside her yearned to please Gregory in a way she had never wanted to please another lover.

As she lowered her mouth to Gregory's penis and heard his corresponding gasp, she tasted the truth on her tongue. She hadn't been content, she'd never been content. She had simply never met a man who had awakened her desires the way Gregory had. At the core of her frustration was the knowledge that she wanted as much as he did—she wanted all the possibilities, all the variations, all the dirty, naughty things a good girl like her was never permitted to want.

She dared to peek at him from under her lowered lashes and saw that he was watching her. The knowledge should have intimidated her, but instead it emboldened her. She took more of him into her mouth, cradling him in the hollow of her tongue and tasting his arousal as it leaked from him.

"Ohh," he sighed, a long drawn-out sound of pleasure as she drew him to the back of her throat and held him there.

Kneeling there with his dick in her mouth, she remained still and waiting. Wanting him to give her what he promised. Wanting the hardness and roughness that her body craved. She held him in her mouth, her tongue, lips, and throat caressing him. Then, as if he couldn't control himself, he flexed his hips until only the head of him remained between her lips before thrusting into her mouth.

She groaned around him, wanting exactly this. Only he took it as a sound of protest and withdrew from her mouth, studying her with concern.

"I'm sorry," he said.

She shook her head. "More," she said easily. "Hard. Rough."

Something flashed in his dark eyes. Something wild and feral, something she desperately wanted him to unleash on her.

"Now," she said, crisp and firm. And then, softer, "Please."

He held himself in his hand and pushed the tip of his dick between her lips once again. This time, it was he who controlled the motion. This time, he pushed to the back of her throat until she nearly gagged. This time, he gave her exactly what she craved.

"Like that, baby?" he asked, though he had to know her answer by the way she gripped his thighs and moaned.

"Good girl," he said. "Take it all."

She did take it all, and not just to please him. Gregory's dick in her mouth was both her submission and her liberation. She sucked him as she never had before, with wet slurping unlady-like sounds, with whimpers of pleasure and a clenching between her legs. She needed him there, soon. She needed to be filled with the brushed velvet hardness that filled her mouth.

Gregory fucked her mouth as she'd requested, hard and rough, until her throat felt raw and his thighs trembled beneath her touch at the effort it took to keep from coming. She was tempted to let him finish this way, to complete her act of submissive love. But he made the decision for her, slowly withdrawing from her mouth, his erection glistening wet and beautiful.

"I want to fuck you."

She nodded, feeling as if she could smell her own arousal.

"Tell me you want me to fuck you," he said, kneeling on the floor in front of her, guiding her back onto the rug.

Her lips felt swollen, and along with his sweet musk, she could taste the iron tang of blood where she'd protected his delicate skin from her teeth and managed to cut her own lip. The proof of her newfound sensuality. And yet, she couldn't say what she wanted.

Gregory knelt between her thighs, stripping off her jeans and panties roughly. Then his shirt, her shirt, her bra. Until she was splayed before him in the sun splashed room, naked and wanting.

"Tell me to fuck you," he said again.

She caught her breath, willing the words from her lungs. There was nothing but silence. She arched her back, hoping to entice him with her body, hoping he would spare her the embarrassment of saying the words.

"Fine," he said, taking up the paint brush from where it had been discarded on the floor. "I'll show you want I want."

He licked the tip of the brush as she had, his broad tongue gliding over the sable hairs and making her whimper. He dipped the brush between her thighs and traced the lips of her swollen pussy. The gentle touch of the brush tickled, made her aware of the sticky wetness that felt like it was trickling down between her legs.

He traced her pussy in gentle circles, avoiding her clit and the wetness between her lips. She squirmed and whimpered, legs spread and knees bent, utterly shameless in trying to get him to penetrate her or stroke her hard clit. He stubbornly refused, painting around her wetness, teasing her.

"Is there something you want to tell me?"

She growled in frustration, not even recognizing her own voice. "Yes!"

"Well?" he asked, brush poised over her undulating mound.

"What do you want?"

"Fuck me," she said, her voice ragged.

"Hmm," he said with deliberate consideration. "Here?"

She felt the brush at her opening, teasing the wetness that pooled there. She arched her back, taking the brush bristles into her, feeling the paintbrush slip inside her. It was too narrow to offer any relief, but she cried out at the sensation.

"Naughty girl," he said, pressing the brush inward, painting the insides of her with her own juices. "Good girl."

"Fuck me," she said again. "Please."

He withdrew the brush. "Not until you come like this."

She didn't know what he meant until he dragged the brush over her clit, painting the aroused little nub with her arousal. She practically came off the floor as the bristles fanned out to cover her clit, at once tickling and arousing. She panted and whimpered, arms stretched over her head, body thrashing before him.

"Will you come?"

She nodded, bunching the rug in her fists as she concentrated on that point between her legs where the paintbrush met her clit and caressed it into orgasm. He dipped the brush between her thighs again and again, catching her wetness on the bristles and gliding it over her clit. She could feel her orgasm building, the still, quiet pool of arousal that had always been there, crashing over her in a tidal wave of sudden, nearly violent release.

She tried to close her legs around the insubstantial brush, but Gregory's hands were there to pin her knees back until they touched the rug, the brush suddenly replaced by the tip of his dick. Her clitoris throbbed against his hardness as she came in rolling waves, screaming and whimpering as he pinned her helplessly to the rug.

And then he pushed her legs back to her chest and slammed into her in one long, hard stroke. She gasped as he buried himself in her so deep her still-tingling clit pressed against the hard ridge of his pubic bone.

Then it was his turn to remain still.

She stared into his eyes, wiggling her hips in invitation, wanting what he was giving her more than she'd ever wanted anything in her life. She felt his dick throb inside of her, but he remained still. She saw the challenge in his eyes, knew what he was waiting for.

This time, there was no hesitation, no embarrassment, no holding back anything.

"Fuck me," she pleaded. "Fuck me hard, Gregory. Please. I need you to fuck me so hard."

And then he did. Arching up over her, pinning her hands above her head, he fucked her one long, hard stroke after another. She could hear her wetness as he fucked her, the obscene sucking sounds of her pussy drawing him in before he slid out to the tip and thrust back into her.

She pulled her knees up to her chest so he could go as deep as she could stand, feeling his balls slapping damply at her ass, covered in her sticky wetness. His dick filled her up, leaving her breathless and aching, wanting more.

"Good girl, good girl," he breathed in her ear. "Take it all. Take my dick like a good girl."

She pushed against him but was effectively pinned to the floor by his hands and his dick, getting fucked just as hard and rough as she'd asked for. She could feel her arousal building in the pit of her stomach like a knot being pulled tight. She clenched her muscles around his dick, her walls rippling along the length of him, pushing them both over the edge. Her stomach cramped painfully for a moment, and then there was sweet release, a gush of wetness from both of them as she screamed her release into his hard, unrelenting chest.

He kept driving into her as she whimpered and begged word-lessly, craving more and more and more. He fucked her until there was almost no friction because of all the wetness, until he started to go soft. Then he braced himself over her and looked at her sex-flushed face.

His expression was so serious, she had to smile. At that, he smiled back and bent to kiss her.

"Was that, was it—?" Before he could get the words out in a coherent sentence past his own ragged breath, she was already nodding.

"It was exactly what I wanted. It was perfect."

He rolled over, pulling her with him until her head was nestled in the crook of his shoulder, her body flung across his. "Yeah, it was."

"Just like that," she said, pressing a kiss to a bite mark she hadn't even realized she'd left on him. "Every time. Always. Fuck me just like that."

"Hey, you said it," he said, sounding startled.

She laughed. "I'm going to try to say a lot more things," she promised. "I'm going to try to tell you everything that's in my head."

He reached to the edge of the carpet and retrieved the paint-brush. "Well, if you can't find the words, you can always use this," he said, tickling her spine with the bristles, gliding down her back until the tip of the brush nestled in the cleft of her cheeks.

She giggled and squirmed, feeling two things at once—the stir of his penis against her hip and a renewed tingling of arousal between her thighs.

"Tell me what you want," she said. "Tell your very bad good girl how you want to fuck her."

He put the paintbrush down and did exactly that.

NO SLEEP

Kristina Lloyd

He said he wouldn't sleep with her because he didn't want to get emotionally involved. This was a sex thing, nothing else, and he needed his distance if he were to keep seeing her as his dirty little slut. She agreed and said she didn't want to spend the night with him either. If she saw too much of his nice-guy side, she might struggle to believe in that dark, rough brute who glowered and snarled as he fucked her.

But, like everyone, they were busy people, and the no-sleepover rule got problematic. Worse, they lived fifty miles apart so spontaneity wasn't an option. Half their relationship ("If you can call it that," he said, not unkindly) was conducted via email, Skype, and dirty phone calls.

They hadn't seen each other for a month. He had a cold, she had heaps of work on, he had family visiting, the usual. She suggested they meet midway in a hotel for an afternoon. No sleepover. They must have hotels in London where you can pay by the hour. You know, like those Japanese love hotels?

But London, she discovered, is not Tokyo. She complained she felt like a whore, contacting hotels to enquire about hourly rates. "Well don't bank on not being treated like one," he said, making her try a little harder.

Eventually, she found somewhere, booked a room for an afternoon. "So seedy," she said excitedly.

The night before she could barely sleep. Fifty miles away, neither could he. In the morning, she took extra care over her appearance. It had been six weeks. That deserved lip liner, at least. He selected underwear she liked, jeans his arse looked good in, the jacket she'd once admired. He shaved his head because she found it hot when he looked nasty and mean. He glared at himself in the mirror, turning his swag on. He was dom, but he liked to please. She'd told him it wasn't unusual.

She arrived first, checked in, dumped her bag of kit in the room. They met downstairs in the hotel bar, a warm but spacious area with leather sofas the color of good cigars, open fires, bare boards, and red brickwork. Firelight rested on thin metal sculptures and glossed the floor with amber puddles. Behind the bar, rows of tawny-hued spirits gleamed as they might in a country pub, a dangerous enchantment of nectars. It didn't feel like noon.

"See?" she said. "I'm a high-class hooker."

"We'll see about that," he replied, grinning.

They drank brandy, smirking secretively but saying little because there was too much to say and not enough time. Before long, he said, "I want you to go up to the room, strip to your underwear and kneel. I'll follow you in five."

She took her brandy, feeling it was important to carry the magic of the bar to the privacy of their room. He watched her arse as she walked away, wanting to slap it. Upstairs, she drew the curtains, blocking out the rarely glimpsed underside of the

city, the back ends of shabby buildings, delivery doors, and
fire escapes. The room, like the bar, was warmly minimalist,
a cocoon of cream, browns, and aubergine. She turned up the
dimmer switch, stripped and knelt, pleased that the thread of
ribbon in her black bra was a near-perfect match for the bruise-
purple stripe on the bed linen. Not that he would notice. Not
that she cared. This was a sex thing, not a matching-bra-and-
bed thing.

On the dressing table, the brandy glowed like a tiny fireplace. *I could be anyone,* she thought.

When he entered, he glanced at her as if she were nothing
but furniture before he turned to hang his jacket in the alcove-
cum-wardrobe. "Clasp your hands behind your head," he said,
removing his shirt.

She did. She felt nervous and stupid, playing this game of
make-believe because it aroused them. Children play games, not
adults.

He removed all his clothes, aimed the TV remote, then
flicked through screens of information. Naked in the dimness,
he was glorious, his cock erect, vulgar and shameless, his arms
sculpted with light and shadow, his butt taut and lean. Colors
from the TV shimmered on his chest.

She recalled him once telling her about a program he'd
watched, something involving Romans and their servants, and
how it had turned him on. This was months ago when they'd
first started seeing each other (if you could call it "seeing"). She'd
treasured the snippet because he never revealed much about his
day-to-day life. Then again, neither did she. Distance.

But this was cheeky: six weeks apart and he switches on the
TV first? She was aching for the warmth of his skin, the scent of
him and the wild thrust of his cock, and knew he was equally
hot for her. She admired him for being such a cool bastard. The

more he ignored her, the more humiliated and horny she grew. She liked to claim she wasn't ashamed of her kinks, but when she was in the thick of it, compliant, needy, and submissive, she felt embarrassed by the enormity of her lust. She wanted satisfaction and didn't like to dwell on how low she might go to achieve it. But it was a tricky business, this game playing, because going low was part of her pleasure. She loved what she hated, hated what she loved.

He didn't have that problem. He loved it all.

He set down the remote and addressed her. "Hey, what's this? Free whore?"

She winced at his jaunty tone, hated it.

He approached. He had a pen in his hand, a Sharpie. "Now *this* is what I call room service," he said. "What are you?"

Her voice was soft. "A whore."

"Sort of a whore?"

She closed her eyes. "A free whore."

"That's right. Likes getting used so much she doesn't even want paying."

He wrote the words across her chest in black ink: FREE WHORE. She held still, swaying only slightly.

"Arms folded behind your back," he said. He pushed her bra straps down, lifted her breasts free, and grabbed her by the hair. Holding her head firm, he drove into her mouth, increasing his reach until her throat was opening to clasp the last inch of him, so warm and tight. She gazed up obediently, her lips around his root, her eyes watering. Her makeup ran, making her tears as black as the words on her chest.

When she needed air, she tapped his thigh and he withdrew. "Aw," he said, thumbing away a tear. "Such a good submissive." She thought he was taunting her; then, in a gentle voice, he added, "You're beautiful when you cry, you know?"

She thought he was being sincere. (He was.) "I'm not crying," she said.

"You will be soon," he warned.

He was right, of course.

In her bag of kit, she had rope, cuffs, flogger, blindfold, ball gag, bit gag, butt plug, vibe, condoms, lube, Wet Wipes. The crop had been too long to pack, so she'd left that at home rather than have its handle poking out of the zip on the Underground, letting everyone know she was a pervert. She should have left the whole bag at home. All he used were the condoms plus the pen that he'd brought himself. It was testament to his dark imagination he could reduce her to a sobbing wreck with so little equipment.

He fucked her on the bed with slow cruelty, easing himself into her without hitting home. He didn't thrust, he didn't go deep, and the angle was weak. She was on her side, a leg in the air, pleading for more.

"When I'm ready," he said, rocking calmly into her cunt.

She shifted position, trying to take more of him, but he laughed and readjusted, denying her the advantage. "What are you after?" he asked. "Tell me, I might give it to you."

She muttered obscenities, begging him to fuck her and fill her and let her have his cock, oh please, it's torture, I can't stand it, give it to me hard, please, please.

He took the pen, made her twist forward, then wrote her words on her back as if she'd been dictating. "In case I forget what you want," he said. He swiveled her onto all fours, gripped her hips, and penetrated her with one neat, clean thrust. Her walls stretched to take him, and the two of them groaned in unison. "Oh, I've missed this little cunt," he said.

He fucked her one way for a while before flipping her over, pushing her legs back and slamming in deep again. He went at her with a dour force and passion, his face clouded with absorption in the moment, sweat sprinkling from his forehead. She clung to his cock, slippery and snug, and he filled her with his big, meaty aggression, calling her names through gritted teeth. He withdrew without coming—time for something else now—and told her to kneel on the bed.

Her legs were shaky, and she was bothered by the ink stains on the sheets. She imagined the words printed backward on the cotton, entertainment for the chambermaids. *Fuck me hard, please, I can't stand it, I need your cock, please, oh god, please, and do you think that will come out with Dreft?*

He'd had plans he'd been mulling over for weeks, plans involving rope and pain, gags and ass-fucking. But he'd found the Sharpie in his pocket on his way up to the room, and he was running with sudden, new ideas. He made her open her knees a little wider then pushed the pen into her wetness. "Grip it," he said. "Don't let it drop."

"Oh christ." She squeezed her PC muscles, her entire body tensing with the effort. But the pen was so slim, and his cock had been so big, leaving her wet and open. A lifetime of Kegels couldn't have saved her. She couldn't hold the pen for a second.

"Try again," he said.

When she failed for a second time, he slapped her face. This was usually the point when she'd start slipping away from him. He could see it in her eyes. He pinched and twisted her nipples, scratched her skin, and she arched toward him, whimpering for more. He circled and rocked her clit, his fist in her hair, stretching her neck taut. She came quickly. His gaze never left her face.

She looked dazed and remote, as if she existed somewhere behind her eyes. He could do anything he wanted when she started to drift, but he was always careful, measuring her reactions, occasionally checking in for a whispered "yes."

She was in a black, swimmy place veined with purple, pinpoints of light growing large and small. She had no words. If he needed it, she would try her very best to say "yes." Sometimes, "yes" was as heavy as a boulder. When she couldn't manage to lift the word, he always understood. He never heard her silence as "no," thank god.

Her hurt her some more, fucked her some more, sank into her throat, then came on her tits. He dragged her to the mirror so she could see what a whore she was.

She saw a monster. Her skin was blotched and raw, black tears streaked her face, and her eyes, pink rimmed and bloodshot, struggled to meet their image. Her hair was a tangle of knots, and on her chest, the nasty, inked letters were smeared with come and sweat.

He thought she was beautiful and brave, allowing herself to be this thing for him, although first of all, she was this thing for herself, wasn't she? He knelt with her, licked his come from her tits, stroked hair from her face, and kissed her.

She tasted him, sharp and salty, and held him lightly, his back wet beneath her shaking hands. Then she began to sob, the way she always did after a hard session, and he took her to bed, letting her nestle in the crook of his arm till the tears subsided.

"It's okay, just let it all go," he said, unfazed by her reaction. Her tears, he knew, were tears of release. There was no suffering or shame.

She was grateful he understood, that he didn't freak out the way some men did. She'd explained it to him early on, said this was how it was for her, the tears, the vanishing, and he accepted that. He didn't think she was deranged or damaged. He trusted her.

She liked how he held her, tender and reassuring, waiting for her to surface but never rushing her to be better. They called it "aftercare" as if it were different from caring, and as if the dispensing of it were *his* role alone. But he needed comfort too, not as much as her, but he needed it all the same. He wasn't okay till he knew she was okay, knew she was happy.

She smiled, sniffing, then began to laugh, elated and joyful. He laughed at her laughter, then licked her tears. Side by side on the pillows, they kissed lazily. And she remembered back to when they'd first hooked up. "No kissing," he'd said. He didn't want to get emotionally involved. He regarded kissing as something you did in relationships, not when it was like this, just a sex thing.

"But I like kissing, it's horny," she'd complained, and by their third date, the rule had gone, never to be mentioned again. Because aren't rules made to be broken? But the no-sleepovers, that was set in stone. It would complicate everything if they were to lie together, soft, honest, and vulnerable; if they were to drift apart into their separate dreams and wake smudgy-eyed in the morning, nuzzling close to reconnect. Too confusing, too messy, too dangerous. So, that rule was staying.

They wouldn't break it, they wouldn't sleep together; not for a few more months yet.

CROSSING THE LINE

Dominic Santi

After six months of dating, I knew Therese was the one for me. But it took me four more months to pop the question. Despite the exasperated advice of my legal-shark best friend, my cold feet had nothing to do with my six-figure annual income. Hell, Therese made more than I did!

What had me pacing the floor of my townhouse at all hours was the certainty that since I really did want to marry Therese, I had to figure out a way to tell her about my cross-dressing. At five-feet-eleven with curly blond hair and sky-blue eyes, I'd been told I was a good-looking man. However, with feminine attire draped over my slender frame and mascara darkening my long, thick lashes, I knew I made a stunning woman. Eventually, five martinis into a night that ended with Therese and me dancing cheek to cheek and cock to belly on her patio, I blurted out that I loved her and wanted to fuck her senseless every day for the rest of my life—*and* I really needed to occasionally, okay, fairly frequently, dress up in a skirt and heels and the sexiest lingerie I could find on the Internet.

Imagine my shock when Therese cupped my face in her fingers and arched her belly into my erection. Therese was all about lush, sexy curves and dark wavy hair that cascaded down her back. As usual, she didn't hesitate to speak her piece.

"I can't wait to see you in a designer gown. I bet you're gorgeous." She ground against my cock until I groaned. "But from now on, sweetie, you'll be getting your feminine attire right here in town from Martine's Boutique. Friday night is going to be accountability night at our house. I'm going to be present when you try on every item, so I can be certain your delectable derriere is properly presented when I bare your bottom for your weekly corporal punishment session."

My tongue-tied gawking had nothing to do with the liquor. I'd never heard of what Therese called a "disciplinary wife." She assured me that from this day forward, the term was going to be an important part of my vocabulary. She rocked her warm, soft belly against me, stroking her thumbs down the sides of my face as she explained how the next morning she was going to give me the list of rules that would govern our lives. We'd talk about them, and she'd answer all my questions and concerns.

The bottom line—all puns intended, Therese assured me— was that every Friday night, whether we went out to a classy restaurant or had pizza at home, I'd be "dressing" for dinner. Sometime before bedtime, Therese would call me on the carpet to answer for that week's misbehavior. Then she'd lift my skirt, take down my panties, and thrash my lovely bare bottom until it was red and hot and I was crying so hard I was dancing on my high-heeled toes and my mascara was running.

"You're not to worry about your makeup during your punishment, sweetie. When a naughty girl is getting a good, sound thrashing, her mascara runs and her lipstick gets smeared. After corner time, you'll sit on a pillow on the vanity seat and we'll get your face all pretty again. But during your thrashing, you're to concentrate only on how much your bottom hurts and how very sorry you are for displeasing me. Afterward, you may apologize and promise to do better and plead for forgiveness."

I was still stuck on her first sentence. "You're going to *spank* me?!" I was so stunned I would have stopped dancing if Therese hadn't been moving so seductively against me.

"Not spank," she whispered, sliding her hands down my body. Her kisses were hot and full of tongue. I shivered when her fingernails stroked my behind. "I'm going to thrash your lovely bare bottom with my hairbrush." I jumped at her slap. "And young lady, when you're really naughty, you'll wear a big sturdy anal plug as well."

Therese ground against me again, and I came in my pants.

We were to be married two months later. Stone-cold sober, Therese and I had negotiated, in writing, the rules that were going to govern the first year of our lives—the way we would renegotiate every year on our anniversary from then on. Just reading the document made my cock stiffen, even as a cold shiver of sweat ran down the back of my neck.

The first part of the rules covered what Therese called "common sense." I was to obey all governmental laws, with the caveat of being allowed to participate in football and basketball pools at work. Financial, social, and job-related decisions were to be made jointly, with Therese having veto power if she decided I wasn't being "sensible."

The rest of the list brought home to me the reality of what being married to a disciplinary wife meant. Therese promised to be fair and reasonable, to encourage me in exploring my feminine side, and to never wait beyond Friday night to punish me when I'd transgressed. I promised to obey her and to accept a bare-bottomed "thrashing" whenever she decided I needed one. I could discuss any issues that came up, and I was to let her know if I had concerns. But when Therese gave an order, her word was law.

Just picturing the list in my head made my cock fill. She'd listed several specifics to be certain I was clear about them. Disobeying or lying to her, even by omission, was grounds for an immediate thrashing—in addition to the one I'd get with my weekly accounting. That meant even if she hadn't caught me breaking a rule, I still had to confess—or take double the original punishment when she found out.

I was to be in bed no later than fifteen minutes after she was each night. I was allowed to keep my porn subscriptions and my extensive collection of what she called "exceptionally raunchy videos," but I could not masturbate without permission. That didn't mean just not coming, either. I was allowed up to a half-dozen long, slow, soapy strokes in the shower. Anything more than that needed Therese's permission—*before* I did it.

Finally, starting the week after our wedding, I was to leave work early enough on Fridays to stop at the "specialty" day spa next to Martine's on my way home. Therese was leaving standing orders for me for a full-body shave with bikini wax. My face heated every time I thought about that part, so I concentrated on how I was also to get a manicure and pedicure (my choice of colors for the nail polish) and have my hair done. When I left, I'd be carrying a garment bag that now held my suit and tie and the other masculine accoutrements I'd shed before donning the feminine attire Therese had left at the spa for me earlier in the day.

By the time our wedding rolled around, I had a trousseau every bit as stunning as Therese's. Designer dresses, handmade lingerie, silk peignoirs, and gorgeous shoes and bags. I'd even survived my preliminary trip to the spa the day before the wedding. My embarrassment at the specialty extras Therese had ordered for me had quickly faded to blushing excitement when I realized that under my tuxedo, I'd be taking my vows wearing silk panties over my now satiny-smooth crotch.

I made it through the ceremony okay. My behavior at the reception wasn't entirely stellar, but I chalked that up to wedding jitters and at the ribbing I'd gotten because more than one person had picked up on the "obey" in my wedding vows. The few times Therese tapped my butt and warned me to mind my manners, I told myself she really just wanted to fondle my panty-clad backside through my starched black trousers. Although I looked pretty good in my tuxedo, I knew it paled in comparison to my statuesque beauty in the perfectly tailored feminine attire Therese had packed for our honeymoon.

Imagine my surprise when I woke up the next morning in Maui to find myself alone in bed. A piece of white parchment paper with thick black lettering was prominently positioned on the nightstand under Therese's large, oval, polished maple hairbrush. The list started with being rude to the matron of honor and ended with disobeying Therese by drinking an unauthorized third glass of champagne. My hand shook a little as I realized that according to the rules we'd negotiated, I was in for some serious consequences!

Therese walked in from the balcony just as I finished reading. She was wearing a sheer white peignoir that matched the one she'd packed for me. The sunlight from the open doorway silhouetted her gorgeous curves. I swallowed hard, trying to focus on anything but how much I wanted to fuck her. And how nervous I was getting. I pointed indignantly at the paper.

"I wasn't drunk!"

Therese raised her eyebrow. "I'm certain your punishment

list says you were disobedient, not drunk."

It did, but I still didn't like the way the words looked on the paper. I took a deep breath, settling my butt firmly on the edge of the bed and trying not to fidget. "I don't think you should, you know...spank me." I swallowed hard. "I only had a few drinks."

The look on Therese's face made me feel like a bug on a pin. I lowered my eyes, clenching my butt and concentrating on the pattern in the carpet as she walked over to me.

"I know you weren't drunk, sweetie." Therese's fingers were cool and soft against my morning stubble. I sighed and leaned into her palm.

"While I will thrash you in the future if you get drunk without permission, your first bare-bottomed session with the brush will be solely to remind you that I am now your wife. You will always obey me."

I started to pull away, but her light tap on my jaw had me freezing in position. "The rest of your punishment will wait until Friday night. But right now, you need to learn what 'obey' means. I'm going to run a bubble bath for you while you shave everything you can reach. Then you're going to relax in the tub and think about what we've negotiated while I lay out your clothes for you."

I could reach everything but my back. By the time I was done, the huge, heart-shaped tub was overflowing with rose-scented bubbles. I climbed in and leaned back with my head on the bath pillow, letting the water soothe away my anxiety. The extra level of nudity had my freshly shaved skin tingling as I moved against the warm, scented water. I slowly stroked my cock—exactly six times. Just as I was finishing, Therese walked in with my attire. Instantly, my cock pointed up through the bubbles. I wrapped my hand around my shaft again, sneaking in two extra strokes beyond what I was allowed.

Even without the sunlight in back of her, her peignoir clung so I could still see her curves and the dusky shadows of her nipples. She hung my new skin-tight pink minidress with the scoop neck on the back of the door and draped my lingerie across the vanity: a strapless padded white satin bra with matching panties, a lacy white garter belt, and silk stockings with a seam up the back. She set my makeup case and jewelry box in front of the mirror, next to a flowery silk neck scarf. Then she held up my strappy pink stiletto heels, custom dyed to match my dress, so I could admire them before she set them on the floor.

"Lean forward, dear, so I can get your back. Then you can towel off and lotion your entire body."

I couldn't wait to see if the water made Therese's peignoir transparent. But when she put the razor down, she didn't have so much as a drop on her clothes.

"Join me when you're dressed, sweetie. Full makeup. Panties over the garter belt and stockings. And don't tape your penis. Your panties are designed to hold it in place until I take them down for your spanking. Oh, and wear your pearls."

She ran her finger over the side of my naked bottom. I shivered hard. Then the door was closed, and I was alone.

I thought about stalling. But my beautiful clothes were waiting for me. I was also pretty sure that no matter how long it took me to get ready, Therese would be there with that stupid brush. I climbed out of the tub and toweled off. Then I picked up the garter belt and ran my fingers over the exquisitely designed lace.

Therese hadn't ordered me to hurry. I moisturized every inch of my hyper-sensitive skin—except my cock. I'd already pushed my luck there with the extra two strokes in the tub. Then I slid my lacy, snow-white garter belt around my waist. I sat down on the vanity chair, and I lifted my right foot. I pointed my toes, admiring my shell-pink polish as I eased the first stocking on. I shivered as the silk slithered up and over my freshly shaved calf. Walking five miles a day is boring as hell, but it pays off in aces when I arch my legs to show them off under my skirts. I clipped the first stocking into place, then slid on the second.

My cock was poking up in a most unladylike manner. With all the hair shaved away, my manly attributes looked even bigger than usual, especially with how turned on I was. I did my best to ignore them, frowning as I hooked the second stocking in place and stood up.

Therese had assured me the satiny white panties would hold everything properly out of the way. A white pouch that appeared much too small to accomplish its mission was strategically positioned in front. I slid the panties on over my stockings and garters, my eyes widening as the soft silk encased and lifted—and covered my cock and balls. My manly parts were all still in there, but the lines of the panties disguised my telltale bulge in a way that drew even my eyes away toward my legs and bottom.

I gave myself a couple of tentative squeezes. The panties got noticeably tighter, but the outside lines stayed the same. Grinning like an idiot, I stretched my arms high over my head, turning to admire my profile in the mirror. No matter which way I turned, the curve of my tight, round, and very shapely rump was prominently displayed. I tried not to think too much about why Therese was going to be fixating on that particular portion of my anatomy, concentrating instead on looking womanly. This was going to be good!

The thickly padded strapless bra matched the sleek, soft panties. I was surprised to find a plastic bag with a pair of rubber gloves and a small squeeze tube tucked in one cup. A note in Therese's firm, flowing penmanship stated succinctly, "A pretty girl secretly enjoys the feeling of appearing in public with very sensitive nipples. Smear half the tube on each, then rub and tug on both for one full minute. You will then throw away the gloves and immediately put on your bra. From that point on, only your wife may touch your breasts!"

I carefully unscrewed the top. Whatever was in there smelled vaguely like sports cream and candied ginger. I put on the gloves and dutifully squeezed half the pungent, clear gel on each nipple. The gel was cool at first, gradually heating as I rubbed, though it didn't really get hot. I liked the way it made my dusky rose flesh glisten and the tiny tips peak. Sixty seconds later, I tossed the gloves and tube in the trash and worked the close-fitting bra into place.

Again, I had to grin at how delectable I looked. I turned my profile to the mirror, running my fingers up and down my sides as I admired my now very feminine profile. My hands kept coming back to my breasts, lifting them, trailing my fingertips over the thick padding covering my very sensitive nipples. Even through the padding, I could feel the heat of my fingers stroking.

My eyes widened as I realized the heat was actually on my nipples, not sinking in through my bra. I shifted my shoulders, but my bra fit too closely to scratch the itching burn that was building—and not just on the tips of my nipples. Everything the gel touched needed attention.

And only Therese could touch me. My cock strained into my panties as I dutifully lowered my hands and set about finishing dressing. The dress fit me like a second skin, the delicate pink bringing a gentle flush to my skin, the perfectly cut scoop neck enhancing the illusion of cleavage. Damn, my legs looked miles long in those stockings! With each step, my now perfectly lady-like bottom swayed seductively.

I took a long time with my hair and makeup, shifting my shoulders in a vain attempt to soothe my nipples as I brushed the shoulder-length curls of my favorite blonde wig just so. I added especially sultry touches to my face with extra mascara. I outlined my lips with deep rose lipstick until they looked full and pouty. Then I fashioned my scarf around my neck until my Adam's apple was completely disguised, added the matinee-length pearls Therese had given me for a wedding gift, and strapped on my stiletto heels. This time when I turned in front of the mirror, I had to admit my unexpected blush and the way my shoulders occasionally moved on their own in response to the heat on my nipples were definitely enhancing my looks—in addition to keeping me exceptionally aware of the naked parts of my body hidden beneath my clothes. I looked stunning from every angle.

Therese was waiting for me by the sliding glass door. The sun streaming in behind her outlined her curves in luscious detail through the shimmering silk of her peignoir. She took one look at me, and her face broke into a beautiful smile.

"Darling! You look enchanting!"

I blushed and walked slowly toward her, my head high and my hips swaying as I placed one high-heeled foot in front of the other. When I was almost next to her, she took my hand and led me out onto the balcony. Two crystal glasses of sparkling water with lime wedges waited on the table—next to that fucking piece of parchment and Therese's hairbrush. My heel caught in the carpet and I grabbed her hand. Therese patted my fingers reassuringly and, as soon as I'd regained my balance, led me the rest of the way to the table. My face heated and my nipples burned as she motioned me to one chair, then took the other.

"Do you like your panties?"

"Yes, Ma'am. They're very comfortable, and they keep my panty line smooth, even though I'm really turned on." I wasn't sure why the "Ma'am" slipped out. It just seemed like the thing to say, given what was on the table.

Therese nodded, her hand moving lightly over the edge of the brush. "Ma'am is an appropriate way to address me at punishment time. By the way, you'll wear different panties after your thrashing—ones that will keep your mind on your very sore bottom rather than your very horny cock, though you're to tell me immediately if you feel undue discomfort on your genitals. Do you understand and agree?"

My face heated more as I shifted my shoulders and tried not to look at the hairbrush. "Yes, Ma'am." Damn, my voice was breathy and feminine in a way I'd never been able to produce before. Then again, I'd never been waiting for a spanking from my wife before!

"Very well. While today's thrashing will address only your need to learn the meaning of the word 'obedience,' we'll go over the rest of your list to remind you what to expect at this Friday's punishment session." She motioned toward my glass and picked up the creamy white paper. "Drink up. I want your vocal chords wet enough for some good strong yells when I'm thrashing you." She took a long, slow sip of her water, pursing her lips as she shook her head at what even I could see was way too many lines of writing. "Oh, dear. You've been quite naughty! Is there anything else you'd like to tell me about before we begin?"

I shook my head, my curls brushing against my shoulders as I forced myself to swallow the cold, wet liquid. I hadn't realized how dry my mouth had gotten. I knew what was on the list. It started with my being rude to her bitchy matron of honor, then ran the gamut from using the wrong fork with my salad to posing with my tie askew for some impromptu pictures.

Therese and I had agreed when we'd negotiated this year's rules that since I was so very serious about being seen in public as an elegant woman, neglecting my manners or decorum at any time would be a punishable offense. The last item was disobeying Therese and drinking that stupid third glass of champagne at the reception.

My hands were trembling, so I set my glass firmly on the table. "Will today's s-spanking be my actual punishment for disobeying you at the wedding? Or is this, um, more general?" Shit. Stumbling over my words was very unladylike.

Therese quirked her eyebrow at me. "Do you need two spankings for disobedience?"

"One would be okay!" Damn. I was even more upset about the tremor in my voice. Therese's fingers were absently stroking the brush now, caressing the smooth, flat, highly polished back. My nipples were burning so much I couldn't help fidgeting. I told myself it was purely because of the effects of the gel, not because I was getting so nervous.

"Very well, dear." She finished her water and motioned for me to do the same. When our glasses were both back on the table, she picked up the brush in one hand and held the other out to me. "Come inside. I'm going to thrash your bare bottom until I'm convinced you've learned to obey your wife."

It had been a long time since I'd teetered on my heels, but I did, every step of the way as I followed Therese back into the room. She shut the door firmly behind us and drew the curtains. Then she peeled off the robe of her peignoir.

The nightgown alone was so sheer I could see the cleft between her pussy lips as well as the clear shadows of her large, dark areolas. She pulled the desk chair out and turned the seat toward me. Then she slapped the flat side of the brush against her palm with a loud *smack!*

"Bend over with your hands flat on the chair. Bottom out, head up so your hair stays in place." As I gingerly took my position, she rubbed the brush lightly over my backside. "Normally, I will have you remove your dress before your thrashing. However, this first time, I want to impress upon you the fact that my husband, even when he is dressed as a lady, will get his bottom thrashed whenever he disobeys."

The first smack caught me by surprise.

"*Ow!*" I stood up, grabbing my bottom in surprise. The look on Therese's face told me that had been a *big* mistake. I quickly bent back down. "I'm s-sorry, Ma'am. I've never been spanked before." I swallowed hard as I gripped the sides of the chair. "I was surprised at how much it stings. I won't get up again."

My voice trailed away as Therese chuckled in back of me. "By the time we're finished here, my love, you will never again be surprised at just how much a thrashing—especially a bare-bottomed thrashing!—can hurt."

"*Ow!*" I jumped as the brush smacked again, but this time, I didn't get up.

"Very good, dear. We shall continue now."

By the time Therese was finished thrashing the back of my dress, I was struggling to hold my position. I was dancing on my toes on the carpet, howling as the brush slapped again and again over my very tender bottom. My wig had slipped, and my face was sopping with tears. My constant litany of "*Ow! Ow! Ow!*" was interrupted only by my profuse apologies and promises to *always* obey her in the future!

The more I sweated, the more my nipples burned. In the position I was in, my bra moved just enough to make the heat in my oversensitized skin itch and flare even more. Therese helped me to my feet and told me to put my hands on my head. As she eased my dress off, I stood there bawling, feeling like a naughty little girl having her bottom bared for the rest of her well-deserved spanking. Therese tugged my panties over my hips.

"I want to keep my panties on!" I closed my eyes, shuddering as I unexpectedly jerked away from her.

Therese froze. Even I was surprised at the panic in my voice. When she spoke, her tone was soft and soothing. "Thrashings in this family are bare-bottomed, sweetie."

"But I don't want my penis hanging out!" It wasn't until I said it that I realized why I was suddenly so upset. I didn't care that my spanking hurt. That was turning me on! I just didn't want my masculine attributes waving where I could see them when I was dressed as a woman.

"Fair enough." She pulled my panties back into place. "Bend over the chair, with your feet spread as wide as the chair legs."

As I carefully balanced myself, Therese opened her makeup kit and took out a tiny, jeweled pocketknife. I held my breath as she slit the back of my panties. The front pouch slipped lower as the fabric gave, but I still couldn't see anything but sheer white satin. The breeze on my backside, however, told me my bottom was now fully exposed. Being spanked by my wife was something I once again wanted—very much.

"We'll buy some appropriate panties at Martine's when we return. Until then, you will hold very still during your thrashings, so this style of panties will suffice."

I did. I wailed and cried and squeezed my bottom cheeks together until I knew, all the way to my bones, that there was nothing in the entire world I wanted to do more than obey and please my Therese!

Afterward, as I stood in the corner sobbing, I choked out my confession to Therese that I'd masturbated two strokes more than I was allowed. I bent over with my hands on my knees and asked her for my punishment strokes. Therese kept her word, giving me six scorching smacks that had me wailing all over again.

I was totally unprepared for my "after-spanking" panties, though. Therese had me step out of the torn remnants. Then she covered my bottom with the same gel as my nipples and pulled a pair of silk tap pants and an old-fashioned girdle over my bottom. As I howled and danced and kept my hands on my head so I wouldn't try to take my "after-spanking" panties off, Therese led me firmly back to the bathroom and plunked me down on the vanity chair.

My bottom burned and my nipples burned, and in the mirror my eyes were glued to the sight of a beautiful and obviously well-spanked woman in her underwear, with her hair in total disarray and her lipstick smeared and her mascara running down her cheeks.

"My b-bottom hurts!" I blubbered, fascinated with how my pouty lips quivered as the tears streamed down my cheeks.

"That's because you've had a big girl spanking. Sit still while I fix your makeup."

As Therese repaired the damage, I fought back my sobs, finally calming down enough to hold a cotton ball beneath my eyes so the fresh tears wouldn't undo her work. When my lips were pouty with color again, I took a deep breath and held perfectly still as Therese brushed on waterproof mascara.

"Maybe I sh-should use that in the future—on punishment days?" My voice wavered, but I wasn't crying anymore.

"No, dear. You'll always wear regular mascara for your thrashings. There's something very special about a girl seeing her mascara run when she's had a good cry—especially when her bottom and her nipples burn. It will help you remember how much you want to obey me." She kissed me gently on the lips.

"Sit here and think about that while I get dressed. We're going out for brunch."

As Therese threw off her peignoir, I smiled experimentally into the mirror—watching her and myself as she took a dress that perfectly complemented mine from the closet. Now that I knew what having a disciplinary wife was all about, I was definitely going to enjoy being married to mine!

A FEW THINGS
TO PICK UP
ON YOUR
WAY HOME

Andrea Dale

Gabrielle," Jake said.

She paused with her hand on the doorknob, attaché case and car keys in hand, professional and sexy in equal measures. "Yeah?"

They'd already kissed good-bye for the day, but he came over to her and slipped his arm around her waist, pulling her against him. Her breasts pressed softly against his chest, and his cock stirred.

He was already half-hard, having planned what he was going to say.

"You know how we were talking about picking up a new toy?" he asked.

A slow smile crossed Gabrielle's face. "Mmm, yes." She wiggled against him a little. He loved how she could get aroused and adventurous just as fast as he.

"Why don't you swing by Eros after work and pick something up?"

"Did you have anything specific in mind?" she asked.

He shook his head. "Give me a call when you get there and we'll pick something out together."

He kissed her again, then let her dash out the door to catch her bus, grateful that he worked at home so he didn't have to face coworkers with a bulge in his pants.

He managed to focus on CAD design all day, but when evening rolled around and he knew Gabrielle would be leaving work, he got distracted. He was ready when the phone rang, comfortable in an easy chair, a printout nearby just in case he needed some ideas.

Thankfully, Eros had a website.

He answered, asked Gabrielle how her day had gone. She bitched a little about her boss, and he let her get it out of her system, make the nightly transition from work to not-work, before he turned the conversation to the sex shop.

"So, did you decide what you want?" she asked.

He smiled. She wasn't quite out of work mode yet, still trying to be efficient and brisk.

"Not really," he said. "I figured we could browse."

He wished he could be there to watch her. She was wearing a raspberry linen suit today, with a choker of pale pink pearls, and the colors suited her dusky complexion and blue-black hair. Beneath it all was an ivory lace bra-and-panties set with matching garter belt. She'd been a pantyhose-wearer when they'd met, and he was pleased that she'd taken his suggestion to try alternatives.

She wore garters exclusively now.

"A new vibrator?" she suggested.

"Tell me what the choices are."

"Jake, I can't stand here and describe—"

"Sure you can," he said, keeping his voice casual. "It'll be fun. Tell me what you see. Tell me what you like."

He heard the catch in her breath. She was figuring out this was a game.

She'd be embarrassed, but she'd get turned on. She could be deliciously uninhibited at home, but outside she still clung to that corporate persona, concerned about how she presented herself.

He was pretty sure he could convince her to play the game, even if she didn't yet realize how much of it he'd been planning.

"They've got them in every color, of course," she said. "I—I like the realistic ones better than the plain, smooth ones."

"Why?"

She was silent for a moment. Finally, "I guess they feel better. Inside."

"Go on," he said. He resisted the urge to touch himself. Not so soon. He was hard, though, thinking about Gabrielle in the store, her cheeks flushing a shade of pink that complemented her outfit.

"I like the rabbit one, but we have one of those," she said.

"So maybe we should think about clit vibes," he said. "Maybe those little ones that go over your fingers."

"Is that what you want me to get?"

She wanted to buy something and get out of there. But he still thrilled to the hint of submission in her question. "I think we're still exploring our options," he said. "What do you think? How would it feel if I wore them and ran my hand all over you? We could get two sets, for both hands. I'd caress every inch of you, get you all trembly before I even touched your clit."

She made a little noise, like a mew. The sound went straight to his groin.

"What's wrong?" he asked.

Very quietly, almost so quiet that he couldn't hear her, she said, "I'm getting turned on."

Not half as much as he was, he suspected. Not yet, anyway. God, he wished he were there with her, so he could touch her, smell her floral perfume. Back her into a corner and bite at the curve of her neck, the specific spot that made her knees weak.

"I'll bet you are, darling," he said. "So naughty, standing in a sex shop fondling all the merchandise. Are your panties wet?"

If he were there, he could slip his hand under her skirt and find out for himself. Feel her slickness, taste it on his fingers.

"Yes." It was a whisper.

"Are your nipples hard?"

"Yes."

"That gives me an idea," he said. "Go find the nipple clamps."

"Oh, Jake."

"I thought you wanted to try them someday."

"Well, I did—I do, but..."

"But you don't want to walk up to the clerk with a pair dangling from your fingers? It's okay, honey, he's seen a lot worse."

Her deep breath was audible through the phone. "Okay. They're in a case, so I can't get too close."

"If there are any we want to look at closer, we can ask to see them," he said as if he were standing right next to her.

"Jake!"

He knew that nothing made her feel more exposed than confessing her kinks to a stranger. Admission bared her soul, stripped her more completely than if she took off her clothes right then and there.

Despite her protest, though, he knew that if he asked her to, she would have the clerk open the case and hand her the clips she pointed to. She was completely divorced from her corporate persona now.

His jeans were too tight. He popped the buttons and eased them down. So hard, just from talking to her, suggesting what she should do.

Hearing her comply.

"Tell me about the clamps," he said.

"They have the clover-leaf kind, and the tweezer kind, and some that look like clothespins."

"They'd all look pretty adorning your breasts," he said. God, but he could imagine that—her dark nipples pouting out between the shiny silver that surrounded them.

"Not...painful ones," she said softly.

"Oh no," he agreed quickly. "I don't want to hurt you. Just excite you. Just light clamps that would make you more sensitive. Maybe ones with little bells hanging off them, to chime whenever you moved. You'd sound like a whole campanile tower going off when you came. Would you like that?"

"No," she said, and his heart sank, but then he heard, "I don't need any help, thanks. Just browsing. I'll let you know if I have any questions."

"Was that the clerk?" Jake asked.

"Yes," Gabrielle said. "I hope he didn't hear anything."

"He didn't," he assured her. "I was the one talking. Did *you* hear my last question?"

"Yes."

"What was it?"

She wouldn't want to answer, not if the clerk was nearby. He hoped she would. He thought she was far enough along in the game, in the mindset.

"Whether I'd like it if I wore clamps with bells." She said it in a rush, almost one long word.

"And would you?"

"Maybe. Should I get them?"

"Or maybe little tiny ones that you could wear to work. Your nipples would be hard all day, rubbing against the lace of your bra."

"I wouldn't be able to concentrate," she protested.

"You would if you went to the bathroom and masturbated when you got too horny to think," he said.

"Oh god..."

Before she had time to process more than her initial reaction, her immediate mental picture, he said, "Go over to the next aisle. What's there?"

The clack of her heels against the floor. Then, "The bondage stuff."

"Mmm. We've got those fun fur-lined restraints already. Is there anything else that looks fun to you right now?"

"There's a lot to choose from." She sounded a little overwhelmed.

He was feeling pretty overwhelmed himself, but for a different reason. This was going even better than he'd planned. He couldn't resist a few light strokes along his hard cock. "What's right in front of you?" he asked.

"Some thigh cuffs, with cuffs for your wrists. My wrists, I mean."

"That might be a fun way to tie you down if I used those finger vibrators on you. Keep you from flying off the bed."

"Jake..."

"What, darling?"

"I...I need to come home now."

He caught himself before he laughed out loud.

Keep the game going.

"Why?"

"I'm horny," she whispered.

"Well, I should hope so. I am, too," he admitted. "I'm so

hard I can barely think. I want you so bad. But we're not done shopping."

She whimpered.

"Just a little while longer," he said, not quite sure if he was saying it for her benefit or his own. "What's in the next aisle?"

"Jake, just let me buy something and—"

He steeled himself, just in case it didn't work, and said, "You keep being so impatient, and I'm going to tell you to buy one of those little egg vibrators and put it in before you get on the bus."

She might scoff. She might just say no and walk out. Maybe he'd taken the game too far.

The silence seemed to stretch on forever. Then, she said, "Paddles and whips and stuff."

He hadn't realized he was holding his breath until she spoke, and it took him a moment to understand she was describing what was in the next aisle.

He filed away the idea of getting one of those bullet vibes, something with a remote control, and playing with it around the house.

For starters.

"Do any of them look fun?" he asked.

"There's a paddle covered with bunny fur," she said.

"I'd bet you'd like it if I rubbed it against you after I smacked your sweet ass with it," he agreed. His groin tightened at the mental image of her tied face down on the bed, a pillow beneath her hips to raise her curvy butt in the air for a better target. His thumb slipped through the bead of moisture at the tip of his cock. "What else?"

"Um...a flail with soft suede strips."

That would sting more than she realized, he thought with a smile. Oh, the marks it would make on her sweet ass...

"I don't like the riding crops or the canes."

"That's fine," he said. "I wanted to decide together what to get."

Once she'd agreed to keep going, he'd known he had her. As tempting as it was to have her stand in front of the butt plugs while he described in excruciating detail how he'd lube her up and fill her ass, he wanted her home.

Wanted to hold her against him, smell her shampoo, to kiss her and tell her how wonderful she was before he led her to the bedroom and brought both of them to the release they both craved.

He imagined her there in the store, legs pressed tightly together against the pressure of her arousal, mortified at the thought of going up to the counter with a basket full of deviant purchases—the clerk and anyone nearby aware of her proclivities—but so overwhelmingly horny at the idea of playing with all the items when she got home.

"I agree with you that the bunny-fur paddle sounds like fun," he said. "Go ahead and get that, and the tweezer clamps, too—they're the most adjustable. Those wrist-to-thigh cuffs. And some lube, whatever looks good to you.

"Then hurry home, darling. It's going to be a long night...."

LIFE LINES

Nikki Magennis

The car park was empty. When he cut the engine the quiet bloomed, so that every noise was audible—the *shush* of their clothes, the *thrum* of her bootlaces as she pulled them through the eyelets, the *thunk* of door bolts as he locked up. Above them early morning bird song laced through the treetops.

"No one here," he said, looking at old tracks crisscrossing the dirt.

"Of course." She looked at her watch. "It's half-six. I think I'm still asleep."

"But we've got the hill to ourselves."

He was right. They were the only ones on the path, just them scrambling through a bare, leafless landscape. Her red jacket was the only bright thing visible for miles.

From a distance, the trees were pale scratches against scrub, but up close, if you looked hard, the thin, stretching branches were starting to color. A willow showed shoots of acid yellow, no buds or leaves yet, but the bark tinged with the first flush of sap, rising from somewhere deep in the wintering ground.

"It might be spring," he said, catching the end of a twig and bending it toward himself like a whip. Jacqueline, close behind and breathing hard, pulled herself upright and looked at him.

"It'll come. No rush."

She looked around the threadbare forest. It was utterly still. Hundred-year-old trees grew silently around them. Her heart bounced in her chest, and her lungs already ached. She hadn't worn enough clothes, just a light shirt and her anorak, zippy Gore-Tex trousers. Waterproof and breathable, she'd thought when she got dressed, not thinking about winds cutting from the northwest or the threat of ice rain.

"Alright?" he said, reaching out to touch her elbow. "Am I going too fast?"

She slapped his hand away, laughing. "I'm tougher than you think. Besides, you were talking about needing to push yourself."

He nodded, looked at the pink in her cheeks.

"Okay. Let's go."

She swung her rucksack over her shoulder.

"Lead on."

They reached the tree line soon after, broke away from the shelter onto the bare mountainside. The path was a cobbled staircase, each step a big boulder. They hit a steady, hard pace and crossed the shallow stream that fanned across the saddle of the hill.

"Not far now," he said, laying a hand on the small of her back, where sweat had soaked her shirt. The warmth of his touch spread and radiated.

"I think I may hate you," she said, leaning over to clear her throat and spit on the ground.

"Tell me at the top."

From there it was a steep climb to the summit. Shale slipped underfoot. The air was sharp, thin gas, breathtakingly cold. They turned onto the peak and looked up to see the world in front of them. Above them, the sky was huge and blank, endless dizzying cerulean. And the hills stretched out, ripples and furrows, ancient old cracks following the fault line that stretched all the way to the North Sea a hundred miles away, as the crow flies.

"Wow," she said. "Beautiful. Almost worth getting out of bed for."

They waited for their heartbeats to slow, felt the sweat dry on their backs as they circled the hilltop, looking for landmarks. Bumping against her elbow, he took her in his arms and they cooried up against the wind, bending into the hollows of one another's bodies. Below them, the surface of the loch glowed sapphire blue. Shadows flickered over the water and across the moor, turning the landscape into a stark kaleidoscope.

"Look," he said, "down, by the fir trees."

Far below them, two deer paced the line of a fence, looking for a way over. As the walkers watched, the deer leapt, cleared the wire in two perfect arcs, and fled across the open grass, white tails flashing.

They tripped down the mountain, her feet sliding on loose pieces of slate.

"Damned shoes," she said.

"Those the ones that are like being barefoot?"

"Yeah. Only much more expensive. You feel every stone."

They reached the turn where the path swerved to follow the stream downhill. A few blaeberries, broom bushes. Mark knelt to drink straight from the burn, cupping his hands for the peat-red water. Jacqueline took a flask out of her backpack. She unscrewed the lid and poured a cup of tea, letting the steam billow into her face.

"Oh, that's good," she said, closing her eyes and sipping. "I could drink this all myself."

"I'm a thirsty man. Give it here."

"Come and get it."

Turning, he grabbed her before she could make a sound. He spun her round, rocked her in his arms. She sucked tea off her lips, squinted at him against the sun.

"You're irresistible when you're angry, did you know that?"

"Hush."

Holding her hips fast, he unzipped her, tugged her trousers down to mid-thigh. Her thighs were shocking white, the hair between her legs jet black, as dense as moss. He tangled his fingers in it.

"What if someone comes?"

"I'll make sure of it."

He knelt on the rock, put his face between her legs and tasted her. Apple and earth. Sharp and sweet. He sipped at her like a bee licking nectar.

"Oh, god."

He slid his tongue inside, as deep as he could, and heard her breath stop. Flicked at her clit. Dug his fingernails into her buttocks, hard, the way she liked it. Scratched at her, meanwhile nipped very delicately around her pussy, tiny bites like an animal testing a leaf with its teeth.

"God," she said, "oh, please."

"Wait," he said, reaching for her wrist. He took her cup and flask and laid them on the ground.

"Hold on here," he said, bringing her hands to the stone ledge of the riverbank, bending her over so that her face was close enough to brush the dirt.

"Okay," he said, and struck her across the arse so hard the sound echoed across the mountainside.

"Oh," she said, clutching at a tuft of undergrowth. She curled her fingers into the hard-packed earth. "Yes. More."

He raked his nails over her skin, left thin white tracks that slowly deepened to red. Hit her as if he was driving her into the ground, alternating slaps with rubs, scouring her so that her skin burned under his hands.

"Push it," she murmured into the sifting wind. "Push me. Fuck me."

He slid his fingers between her thighs, dug into her, up deep inside her where she was scalding hot. The flask was kicked over, the lid rolling away from them, the tea spilling all over the stones and trickling into the river. He pulled his cock out and slid it inside, cupping her marked flesh with his hands, working gently now, kneading her, whispering her name over and over. Opening her like a bruised flower, reaching inside to the sweet, wet depths of her. The orgasm rose from the root of his cock, swelling like a river in spate.

She came hard, doubled over, begging him for something she couldn't name.

Afterward, while Jacqueline chased after the missing lid and fished it out from a clump of pale, dead grass, he splashed his face with ice-cold melt water and looked up at the overhanging willow.

Standing, he pulled at a low branch and bent it back until it gave way. He worked at the green stem until it splintered free. It wasn't easy to break living wood, but it came eventually. He batted the stick against his palm.

"What's that for?" she asked, joining him.

"Later," he said, smiling as he took her hand. They turned toward the path and walked on into the blossoming day.

MARCELLE

Alana Noël Voth

I've eroticized my childhood traumas.
—Stephen Elliott

When I was ten, an ice cream truck drove through our neighborhood playing "Hark! The Herald Angels Sing" in the middle of June, and my brother pulled down his shorts and pissed on my bicycle wheel. It was the beginning of chaos, when I started to twitch, when sunlight pressed me to my knees in front of my bike, and I ran a finger between the spokes of my bicycle wheel. I inhaled the ammonia of my brother's piss and gagged a little, swooned.

That same year, I started to dream someone came in my room while I slept and slugged me in the stomach. I'd wake gripping my gut, then double over and drool off the side of my bed.

My parents sent me to a psychiatrist.

"Ronan, why do you hit yourself?"

I tried to tell him. Didn't matter what I said though. I had an inferiority complex. The shrink explained it to my parents: I felt inferior to my brother.

In high school I had an English teacher who said love stories saved people. Lately, I walked up and down Hawthorne Boulevard and imagined I garnered heat. Marcelle was an ember in bed beside me at night; if light came through a window I saw a disturbance across her face. She complained she hadn't slept well since her teens. Sometimes she kicked off the blankets and then writhed. I bent my body around hers the way she'd told me to, then held my hand below her collarbone, above her breast, and counted how many times her heart struck her ribs. Infinite.

Five months ago I turned eighteen and left my parents' house in suburbia. I had to go; I felt claustrophobic, crazy, except ghosts were like ticks under my skin. I itched. After a week on the street, I crashed at a homeless shelter, then took my first shower in six days. Later, I sat in a corner and ate a sandwich. I had a backpack with me, a few things: this faded three-by-five photo of my brother in his soccer uniform, number 33. He was tall and lean, always beautiful. The perfect martyr asshole.

I folded the picture before I could see much else, then slipped it into my backpack again.

This is a love story. When you tell a love story, everyone wants to know how you met because the genesis of most things is sexy even if it's graceless, Point A, something you can see. I used to walk around looking at the ground so my brother wouldn't say, "You staring at me again, Ro-Ro the Twitch?" Eyes were the windows to the soul.

Five months ago, while walking with my eyes on the ground, I found twelve dollars.

Two days later, Marcelle found me in a bookstore.

"Hey there, hey you, look up."

Between rows of books and a smell of book bindings and coffee, I looked up. No way I couldn't. Her voice traveled the length of my spine, curled around my throat, tightened. There she was, the most stunning girl in the world. Strawberry-blonde hair and red lipstick. The girl didn't smile. She dropped a book to the floor. "Pick that up," she said to me.

Love was holy. Love was a visceral thing. Here was peace. After Marcelle flogged me with such force and attention, I collapsed to the floor, then she blew through her lips at the welts on my stomach. I was so sore, I'd never leave her. She cradled my head. "Thank you," I said.

Six months ago, when Marcelle found me in a bookstore, we were in the erotica section, or maybe it was romance. I could never tell. After I retrieved the book for her and held it front of me I said, "Here," and she looked me up and down a moment.

"Oh, I don't want it," she said.

"Okay." I looked for place on a shelf and tried not to twitch, except it was as much a part of me as the mole on my elbow.

"I like you," she said.

"What?" I studied the bookshelf and twitched.

"I mean I know you."

"What?" I twitched again. "From where?" I looked at her.

"Right here," she said.

"I've never been in this store before." I found space on the shelf and replaced the book.

"Why do you do that?" The girl cocked her head. "Nervous habit? You have that condition?"

I shrugged and then twitched again. "Started when I was a kid."

"Amazing how much starts then." The girl touched my shoulder. "I'm Marcelle."

That was a fantastic name: her name was everything. I stared at the bookshelf in front of me as if the books could compete with this girl. Impossible. Funny. "I'm Ronan," I said.

"Doesn't fit you," she replied.

"What?" I looked at her, twitched.

"Ronan," she said.

I shrugged. "It's Gaelic, means little seal."

Marcelle cocked her head again.

"My brother called me Ro-Ro." Shit. I shouldn't have told her that.

I mean, why did I have to bring up him?

"Ro-Ro?" Marcelle stared into my eyes. "Maybe they both fit."

"I guess."

"What're you up to here?"

I looked around the bookstore. "I was going to...borrow a book or something."

"Borrow?"

I shrugged, then cracked a smile.

"You need a job?"

Twitch. "I don't know, maybe."

"I know a porn shop that needs help."

"What porn shop?"

Marcelle told me.

"Isn't that a gay porn shop?"

"So?" She smiled. I twitched.

To tell you the truth, people often assumed I was gay. My brother was the athlete: I was the faggot. Aside from the fact I was thin and sort of gangly, my hair curled into what my mom once referred to as "ringlets." Death of me. My brother let me have it. "Ringlets? Ha ha. Girls have ringlets. Ro-Ro, the girl." Sometimes I imagined wearing girls' underwear, but I wasn't sure that made me girly or gay or even effeminate, maybe ambiguous. Anyway, I'd never admitted it.

Who could I tell and not be ostracized for life?

"The guy at the porn shop is nice. I know him," Marcelle said.

"Thanks. I mean I've got nothing against gay porn shops. I'm just not gay."

Marcelle smiled then pushed a piece of hair behind her ear. "Where do you live?"

Jesus. Hard questions. You need a job? Where do you live? I'd strike out with this girl any second. "I don't know," I said. "Places, I guess."

Marcelle stepped closer. I saw the pores in her nose, a few freckles; then I admired the bow shape to her lips. "Let's get out of here," she said.

"Okay." I continued to stare at her mouth.

When she started to go I followed. Outside she pointed west. "My place is that way, eight blocks."

I couldn't believe this. She wanted me to go with her? "Okay," I said.

We started to walk. Above us the sky looked dusky as we traveled west up Hawthorne Boulevard, the time of night before vampires came out. Traffic passed us on the street. I wanted to ask if she believed in vampires, things that went bump in the night. She walked with her eyes forward and chin out. No hint of a smile. The foggy dusk light loved her. She was like a movie, all motion and purpose. Here was the city, the place where we met. More depressed people lived in Portland than anywhere else. Mold grew like crazy, and so did the vegetation. The air often smelled like rotting flesh. The Willamette River flanked the city, and the ocean wasn't too far away. We were hound-dogged by fog and clouds most days, and even in summer it rained.

"You've got a masochistic tendency, don't you?" Marcelle finally looked at me. The sidewalk was crowded. She leaned into me. I felt her warmth, caved to the pressure.

We got closer to the curb.

"What do you mean?"

"You know what I mean."

"Like I'm a pussy?"

"Being a masochist doesn't make you a pussy."

I twitched. "My parents sent me to a shrink when I was ten. He said I had an inferiority complex."

"You should never see a shrink again."

"I won't. I mean, I wasn't going to."

"You need someone to give you what want." Marcelle smiled. "Like, I could shove you into traffic right now if you want."

"What? That's crazy. I mean, that's dangerous." And then I think I felt a twitch in my cock.

Marcelle shoved me off the curb; she was strong. I fell backward into the street. A driver honked his horn then yelled, "Asshole!" I leapt back onto the curb. My cock was stiff as a dead man. "Jesus Christ! Jesus!" Suddenly, I was invincible. Maybe this was how it had been for my brother when he'd kicked a winning goal. Yeah. I'd almost pissed my pants. Jesus!

"Want to crash with me tonight?" Marcelle said.

I looked at her still breathing hard, adrenaline. I fell in love with her then.

My brother played soccer in high school and was headed to Olympic greatness. You could have asked my dad. He would have told you. My parents loved my brother more than they loved me. My dad touched him all the time: he'd pat my broth-

er's shoulder, run a hand through his hair. I peeked once at my
brother in the bathroom, naked and golden in front of a mirror,
how he reminded me of Brad Pitt, how distracted he was by his
own beauty, a narcissist. Beside him a radio played a song by
Billy Talent. The words went, "Being great must suck."

My brother glared at his reflection.

Marcelle and I lived on the corner of 54th and Hawthorne in
a house once occupied by a wine steward and his wife who
wrote erotic novels involving S&M. That was why Marcelle had
rented the house. She'd read all the writer's books. It was also
why I had a tattoo on my left shoulder that said *Pain Slut,* the
title of the writer's most popular book.

The night Marcelle stenciled me with a knife, I ejaculated
into my pants.

Pain was a color, violet-red.

Marcelle left kiss marks around her artwork, and then I
collapsed, blissful as I'd ever been.

The writer and her husband had left the states for Europe.
Marcelle and I imagined their travels. We imagined bicycle rides
through the country and patio cafés. We imagined wine and
beer, pasta con sarde and Schweinbraten. We imagined leather
bars and sex clubs. We imagined piss and come and blood. It
was all so romantic. We slept on a bed in a pink bedroom. The
blankets and sheets were varying shades of purple, crumpled-up
blossoms. We had incense and porn. Marcelle had a turntable.
She'd stockpiled records: David Bowie and Blondie and the
Germs. She'd bought them at garage sales and on Hawthorne
Boulevard, specialty shops and thrift stores. Marcelle had
crammed the house with bookshelves and had more books than
anyone in the world. My goal was to read every book she had.

One morning, before she left for work, Marcelle snapped a

cuff around my ankle, then attached the other to the leg of a table. She gave me a copy of *The Story of an Eye* by Georges Bataille and a bottle of water. She also gave me a pan to fill. By noon, I'd pissed twice.

When Marcelle returned home later, we gathered around the pan and gazed into it like a wishing well or something.

"Have you ever imagined drinking piss?" she asked.

I remembered the sting of my brother's ammonia, how the smell of it on my finger had sent me gagging and swooning. "Not exactly." I twitched.

Marcelle curled a hand in my hair. I shivered more than twitched.

The guy who ran the gay porn shop looked like Philip Seymour Hoffman. His name was Cade. He fed me often, usually tacos from up the street, then teased me. "Don't lose your figure." First time I met Cade, he looked me over, then said, "You'll be popular with my customers."

"Okay."

"You've got that whipping-boy look."

"I do?" Marcelle had dyed my curls black. Sometimes she put makeup on me, mascara and eyeliner and electric blue eye shadow. The effect was less goth and more gay.

She'd pierced my ears with a straight pin and ice. She'd snapped a dog collar around my neck with a tag on it: Ro-Ro. She's said she loved how I looked in leather pants. Once she teased me. "My, what a big dick you have." When I said thank you she said, "Kneel." And then I'd knelt an hour with a lump in my pants.

"Sure," Cade said. "You look like Japanese manga. Stick with the tight pants."

"Okay."

At first I did chores around the shop: sweeping and stocking mostly, but the customers kept asking me if I wanted to make tips.

Finally I nodded. "Alright," I said.

The first guy just wanted to watch a porn film and jerk off on me. Cade kept Wet Wipes around. Today he asked, "Do you care if the customers hit you?"

"Nah, don't think so." I got hard thinking about it because I imagined Marcelle watching the guys knock me around. Like a scene. I imagined her saying, "Hit him harder. I want bruises. Give him a nosebleed too." My cock went tight with blood. I felt dizzy.

"You worried about your face?" Cade asked.

"I don't know."

"They could get excited and knock the shit out of you."

"I guess I'm a little worried."

"I'll tell them not to hit the pretty boy in the face." Cade winked.

"Okay. Think I could end up in the hospital?" I'd started to sweat, then I twitched.

"I'll keep an eye on you, Ronan."

"Has anyone died here before?"

Cade shook his head. "Course not, dude."

Twitch. "I like pain," I said. "I just wanted to know." I lifted my arm to wipe my brow. Suddenly I fantasized a tall, meaty faggot slugging me in the stomach before closing his hands around my neck. I saw the fire in his eyes. I saw stars and then white light before it went red. Maybe that was what it was like when you hung yourself with a belt in your bedroom.

I sort of felt sick.

"Hey, Ronan." Cade eyeballed me. "I don't allow any simulated snuff shit. Got it?"

I cleared my head. "Yeah, thanks." I smiled then grabbed a broom.

"Make sure you get that spot in front of the floggers display," Cade said.

I was fourteen when I stood at a mirror in the bathroom I shared with my brother and didn't have a shirt on; I wore only my underwear. My reflection was narrow and white. I had sleep in my eyes; my hair stood on end. I'd just woke from another dream where somebody slugged me. The radio stood silent on the counter beside the sink. My brother had arranged his razor and shaving cream, a bottle of Tommy Hilfiger cologne, and a tub of hair gel beside the radio. My stuff remained shoved in a cupboard beneath the sink. To the left of my ribcage, a sore spot. Another bruise blossomed against the canvas of my skin. Just me and my inferiority complex there.

"I hate my father," Marcelle told me one evening. I wore boxer shorts and a Mr. Happy T-shirt my mom had bought me at Target two years before. I knelt on a throw rug on the living room floor. Marcelle wore a pink and blue nightie. She stopped dancing circles around me to observe my upturned face from above. I wanted to hug her around the legs.

"Why do you hate your father?" I asked.

Marcelle parted my lips with her fingers. She slid two fingers into my mouth. "Suck my cock," she said.

My brother had teased me about the T-shirt. "Mr. Happy?" he'd said. "That's hilarious, you fucking crybaby, Ro-Ro the Twitch."

As usual, I'd stared at the ground and blinked it back and twitched.

"You'll never get girls like that," he'd said.

"Mom got me the T-shirt. It's just a shirt."

"It's gay," my brother had said.

Whenever I went to his soccer games, I'd flinch when he kicked the ball down the field; I'd marvel at his agility and prowess: I'd sit in the bleachers and give way to the sun and melt.

"That's good," Marcelle said to me with her fingers in my mouth. "Make me happy."

Marcelle said the reason she liked her job in the lingerie shop was the old men who tipped her to model the merchandise. Every morning she got into her uniform: a white dress and sandals. She put on lipstick and parted her hair in the middle. The dress was transparent. I saw a silhouette of her legs behind the material. Marcelle wore flower-printed underwear.

"I never give them more than a show," she said one morning. "They're desperate though; they try. I mean, they want control, don't they?" Marcelle looked at me as I knelt on the floor.

"Yeah," I said, and it scared me a little, some old guy getting the best of her.

"I like to be mean," she said.

I shivered.

"People like you are stronger than people like me."

I touched the back of her knee at the hem of her dress. I shook my head.

"Think about it," she said. "Who's stronger? The sadist or the masochist?"

I wanted her to be stronger. That was obvious. I twitched touching her knee again.

Marcelle went to the toilet, lifted her dress, and then crouched above the bowl before releasing her bladder. I listened to the patter of her piss against the water. I imagined it neon-yellow in the bowl. The scent of her ammonia was faint but acidic. I wanted to press my nose to her crotch and inhale it. Marcelle dropped the tissue in the bowl then flushed it. She stepped over me to leave the bathroom. I followed behind. Foggy sunlight illuminated her at the front door. The air smelled like rain behind her. I panicked.

"Aren't you going to cuff me to the table today?"

"You're not working?"

"No."

"Oh." Marcelle thought a moment. "Be good. Why don't you clean the house?"

"Okay." I twitched.

Marcelle waved from the sidewalk.

"I love you," I called to her. She walked away. I twitched. After a moment, I crawled to the front door and shut it. Left to my own devices, what would I do? Well, clean the house first. Then call Cade maybe. "Want me to come in a few hours?" I sat on my haunches. *Who's stronger? The sadist or the masochist?* I wanted to run after Marcelle. *Tell me what you mean.*

I closed my eyes. I saw myself at the porn shop. I saw a handsome faggot knocking me around. Last week, a guy had removed his belt, then hit me in the head with it. Hurt. I'd come home and told Marcelle about it. She'd asked me to describe the scene over and over while she used a vibrator. I was with her in the bed but couldn't see anything but her bare calves and knees and her arm that led to her hand holding the vibrator to her cunt under her nightgown.

I'd gotten hard and embellished the story each time I told it.

The handsome faggot said I looked like a girl. The handsome faggot hit me in the side of the head more than once. The handsome faggot pissed in a corner then told me to kneel in it.

"Oh," was all Marcelle had said before she'd shuddered,

then sagged against me and drifted off to sleep.

My humility brought us both peace.

I'd taken her vibrator and held it to my nose, then licked the oily stain of her cunt.

I'd jerked off imagining a garden of bruises flowering across my gut.

I'd fallen asleep remembering the handsome faggot, what he'd said to me in secret. "Know why I don't admit I'm a faggot? Cuz I'm macho shit. Who'd let me play football then? They'd expect it of you, of course, but look at me: I'm macho shit. Know what it's like to be the macho shit, honey? Terrible. That's what it is."

After Marcelle left for work that morning, I went to the turntable and put on the Germs, then regarded the spinning vinyl like something I'd thought gone forever was back from the dead.

I caught my brother once sitting on the edge of the bathtub naked and holding his foot in his lap. His legs were muscular, sinewy, and covered with short blond hairs. He said, "Look at this." Broken blood vessels snaked the inside of his foot. His toes were misshapen, his ankle bruised. "I hate soccer," he said.

"Why do you do it then?" I regretted the question soon as it was out of my mouth.

I started to twitch.

My brother stood off the tub, all tan shoulders and hands; his cock swung from a bird's nest of pubic hair. His eyes flashed as he grabbed my hair.

"Wait, shit, ouch!"

I fell when he yanked the strands from my scalp. I cowered beneath him.

"Why do you do it?" he repeated. "Why do you do it then?"

* * *

Marcelle came home from work and stripped in front of me, then tossed her underwear at the floor. "Put them on," she said. I stared a moment at the ripple of fabric on the throw rug. I hadn't told her yet. Marcelle put on a pants suit. She looked at me, waiting. "Well?"

I crawled toward the panties, twitching.

We walked east up Hawthorne Boulevard. I wore a pink skirt with a ruffle and flower-printed underwear, my tennis shoes with no socks. My T-shirt said, "Mr. Happy." Same one. Marcelle walked with her arm looped through mine. Hardly anyone looked at us. She took the lead. I felt giddy, like we were walking naked down the street. I was naked. Look at me!

Ahead Marcelle saw a pair of glasses on the sidewalk, abandoned or lost or something. She stooped to pick them up then put them on her face, perched on her nose. The lenses made her eyes appear three times larger than normal.

"Everything's magnified," she said. Marcelle looked through the glasses. She looked adorable like that. "Isn't it weird, the closer things are, the harder it is to make things out?" Marcelle looked past me. "Is that a tree over there?"

"Yeah."

"Take me."

"Really?"

"Let's go."

I studied her a moment. Her expression was cool. "Now," she said. Her mouth twitched in one corner. I took her arm, felt a short line of hairs beneath her elbow. I led her toward the tree through the people; she followed without wavering, like she trusted me.

"You could walk me right into a manhole," she said.

"I wouldn't." My skirt swung against my legs. I liked the ruffle.

"Because you're not mean," Marcelle said. She moved her hand up my arm. She held me.

"You're not mean either."

"Yeah, I am. I pushed you into the street once."

"You measured it," I said. "You knew how close the car was."

"Maybe."

I turned and looked at her. "I love you," I said.

Marcelle blinked at me through the glasses. "You do, don't you?"

"Yeah."

At the tree, Marcelle put the glasses on me. Glorious smudge. Marcelle straightened my skirt. "So sexy."

"Thanks." Giddy again. For a second, I stared into the sun.

Marcelle instructed me to turn and face the tree. She said to wrap my arms around it. I held the tree. Marcelle patted my ass.

"Guess what I have?"

"What?" My cock twitched.

"A dildo."

"Really?" My cock went hard.

"I'm going to lift the back of your skirt," she said. "Then lube you."

"Okay." I hugged the tree. Traffic went by in the street. Marcelle ran her hand across my ass under the skirt. She pressed her finger between my ass cheeks, then found my hole. She lubed me up. The sensation was incredible. I quivered inside the skirt.

"Can I jerk off?"

"No."

"Okay."

Marcelle pushed the head of the dildo at my asshole. "The

man who lets me fuck him is the man for me." Her breath tickled my ear. We were going to do this. She'd do this for me. Marcelle pushed the dildo deeper. I felt my ass open. The dildo filled me. Cars went by. People passed on the sidewalk. My cock throbbed. She fucked me. I hugged the tree and stared up at the leaves, how they'd become one glorious garden green. She found my prostate. Oh Jesus.

"What do you see?" she asked. "Look."

Fuck. Give me a minute. I saw how nobody looked at us. Impossible. We were invisible, no magical, on another plane. Marcelle hit my prostate again. "What do you see?"

I caught my breath, not twitching. "You love me," I said.

Every Friday night she watched this show, *Supernatural*. Two brothers, Sam and Dean, fought evil. The evil things could not defeat them. They were strong; they were bound by blood.

"Love between brothers is holy," Marcelle said. "That bond sticks."

I didn't look at her. I stared at the floor and twitched.

"Ronan?"

Soon enough, I crawled to her. "I killed my brother," I said.

He used to stare at me across the dinner table, a round table with a glass top smudged by fingerprints, the ones I pressed into existence rather than hold my fork or eat. I wasn't hungry for the stuff on my plate. I looked between my parents while Dad went on and on about Aiden, my boy, my son, and he'd project this joy around the table that circled like a hawk before landing on my mom. She'd smile and say, "We're so proud of you. You'll get the *gold*." My stomach kicked up bile: I tasted a ball of it on the playing field of my tongue. My dad's joy took flight again, then reached my brother and settled on his shoulder; it dug in its claws as he stared at me. I decided to keep his secrets for revenge. *He hates soccer. He does it to please you. He's afraid to be less than great.* Amazing. My brother had been so fragile.

Marcelle held me around my head. I pressed my face to her stomach. A piece of her dress stuck to my mouth. Tears drowned my eyes, snot clogged my nose. I was wracked by guilt.

"He hung himself," I said. "I never told anyone his secret, how he hated soccer. I knew and I never said anything. I just let him suffer, I let him hurt me."

Marcelle pet my head. "Look at me, Ronan."

I looked.

"I've wanted to kill myself before," she said.

I hugged her around the waist. "Please don't, please. I love you."

"Of course not." Marcelle hit me so hard I fell sideways. "You're saving me."

WHIPPOORWILL

Teresa Noelle Roberts

A whippoorwill shattered my attempt to sleep, calling out over the lake with a startlingly loud demand that someone beat him. I sprang bolt upright in the narrow camp bed. "I'm going to kill that fucking bird!"

Ben, who'd had the fun of a four-hour drive on top of our shared end-of-the-first-year-of-law-school exhaustion, had slept through the whippoorwill and the other weird, unexpected woodsy night sounds that kept me from sleeping. Hell, he'd even ignored the lumpy mattress that was just as vintage as the rest of the furnishings in our borrowed cabin. But my burst of temper woke him.

"It's nature, Cathy. It's supposed to be relaxing," he murmured, nuzzling at the small of my back. "So relax."

Normally Ben's lips tracing my tailbone and working up my spine would have set me shivering so much that I wouldn't care I was desperately underslept. Sex had gotten us through our first year at Yale Law. Granted, most of it had been rushed, without the energy for bondage, beatings, or any of our shared kinks. Sometimes we'd fall asleep partway through and wake stuck together like dogs.

This week, at his uncle's cabin on a secluded New Hampshire lake, was supposed to recharge us so we had the energy for properly improper sex. But how was I supposed to recharge if I couldn't sleep? I hadn't brought ear plugs. I hadn't thought I'd need them way out here. "Who knew peace and quiet would be so damned loud?" I groused, sliding out of Ben's arms and out of bed.

"You can sleep through car alarms, sirens, and screaming drunks, but not a bird?"

"Those are normal, constant city noises. I can ignore them. But first this place seems spooky quiet and then..." The bird call jarred through the air again. "Some kinky bird starts screaming for kinky love—in the third person, no less. Why doesn't his damned top show up and give poor Will his beating so we can get some sleep?"

I stomped to the kitchen and poured cabernet into a Looney Toons juice glass. Wine might help me sleep, or at least relax me enough that I wouldn't be Grumpy McGrumpypants at Ben.

As I poured, I looked out the picture window. The lake was moon-illuminated, and the sky was domed with more stars than I'd ever seen outside a planetarium. I couldn't see lights from any of the other cabins on the lake.

Okay, there was something to be said for the boonies.

And here, I had a chance for a pleasure a city girl rarely experiences—sipping wine outside stark naked on a lovely night.

Glass in hand, I wandered onto the deck overlooking the lake.

The whippoorwill was still begging for a beating, but under the stars, it sounded more lovelorn than annoying. A light, pine-scented breeze cut the humidity and caressed my bare skin, perking up my nipples and reminding my pussy that I'd left a handsome, naked man alone in bed.

A poor choice, that. A few more sips of wine and I'd rectify that mistake. If nothing else, we could smooch and cuddle, and maybe I could drift off to sleep in his arms.

Before I could, though—before I could even have that next sip—a strong hand plucked the glass from my hand, then bent me forward over the railing.

My ass cocked back in response. I knew that position. I liked that position.

"How long has it been, Cathy?" Ben's voice was full of silken menace. "How long since I've beaten you?"

I shivered and clenched at the memory of pleasures long neglected. "So long we didn't even bother packing toys. Damn it."

"I still have my hands, Cathy. Do you want a spanking?"

The wave of lust that crashed over me suggested I'd been mad at the poor bird because I was jealous "Will" might be getting something I wanted.

The first hard thwack sent fire through my out-of-practice butt. I was still considering whether to submit or squirm away when Ben struck three times in rapid succession.

Submit, definitely submit. I needed that hurt to release the stresses of the last few months, and Ben needed to give it. My ass throbbed already, but the throbbing started a matching rhythm in my pussy. "More," I begged. "Please."

Ben stroked the curve of my ass cheeks, lulling me with gentleness—then dug his fingers in hard. "Do you deserve it? You threatened to kill a poor, horny bird earlier. A bird you might have sympathized with. Not very nice. Only good girls get spanked."

That had always been our game. Good girls got spanked, or maybe flogged or caned or something else painfully yummy. Bad girls didn't get anything.

"I've been good!" I sought desperately for examples. "I did well in school. I came to the north woods because you like it up here. I...I cooked dinner!" Grilling up a couple of burgers hardly made me Rachel Ray, but it was better than either of us managed toward the frenzied end of the semester, when PBJs seemed like gourmet treats.

He pretended to consider, alternately petting and pinching my butt. "All right," he conceded, "but only because I want to."

I thanked him, knowing I'd want to curse him before I thanked him again.

Ben wasn't in the mood to build up slowly. He spanked again and again, his hand hard and hot against my tender butt. He pushed me fast to that place where pleasure and pain blurred, a place where I couldn't think of anything except sensation—of the fire building as his hand blasted into my ass over and over again.

God, it stung.

If he stopped, I'd strangle him.

The breeze picked up, teasing at a trail of moisture trickling down my thigh.

But much as I craved this sweet, hot annihilation, even good pain hurts. At home, on the rare occasions when we had time to play, I'd stifled the urge to scream, knowing I was sure to disturb the next-door neighbor, who worked two jobs and caught naps when she could, or send the undergraduates across the hall into spasms of giggling. Out of habit, I tried to stifle cries of pain and pleasure that would shatter the night.

But the nearest neighbors here were probably half a mile away. If they heard anything, it would be muffled and disguised by distance. They might write it off as an animal in heat.

And that was what I felt like, an animal in heat.

I let go with a roar, and as I roared, I came so hard the stars blurred and swirled around me.

Ben thrust into me as I spasmed, setting off another wave of orgasm and another wave of cries that echoed in the silence. He pounded into me, each thrust pushing me higher. I'd have bruises on my hip bones from slamming into the railing, bruises to match the ones on my ass. In the state I was in, that felt good. My ass throbbed, my pussy clenched and gripped. The noises coming out of me didn't even sound human, but they blended into the wilderness perfectly. Ben, too, was noisy, his curses and grunts building to a crescendo. Finally, he yelled for anyone around to hear, "Come for me. Now. While I..."

He lost his words as he exploded, or maybe I just lost track of them, carried beyond words by the force of my orgasm.

Once we reached stillness again, we wrapped around each other on the battered glider, sharing my wine.

"Listen," Ben whispered.

I did.

I heard nothing.

It took a second to remember the significance of the silence. "No whippoorwill."

"Poor frustrated bird," Ben said. "We scared him off. Or maybe someone finally showed up to give him that whipping."

"Now maybe I can get some sleep," I suggested, but Ben poured some wine on my breast and bent to lick it off.

What the hell. We could sleep all day if we wanted to.

SLAVE SISTER

Vida Bailey

He bends over me as I sit in the chair. The length of silk slips cold around my neck, trails shiver between my breasts. He picks up the ends and begins to tie the knot. I love the sound of the whisper and shush of the cold material as he feeds it through the loop.

"Eyes up, missy."

I snap my eyes back to meet their reflection in the dresser mirror. But I can still see my own breasts, nipples hard and eager, flesh firm and willing. I can still see his hands as he draws the knot tight against my throat. I shift, rubbing together thighs that are wet again. He tips my head back to kiss me.

He eases the knot loose and slips the tie over my head, transferring it to his own collar. I watch him in the mirror as he adjusts the knot, smoothes his collar down. His black hair falls over his eyes and his jaw is new-shaven, but I can still see the shadow beneath. His lips are full and red, and I can feel my mouth swell just looking at them. I stand and press myself against him, mindful that I'm naked and wet between the thighs, and I don't want to get a mark on his immaculate grey suit. He lets me lean my face into his shirt, breathe him in. I swear I can smell the strong, warm muscle beneath his skin.

"I hate it when you go."

He touches my face.

"You'll eat popcorn and watch girl movies and write and work and do lunches and wear woolly socks. You'll have a fine time, Saph, you know you will."

"I do know. I like the space. But I'll miss you anyway. And I'll be lonely. And...horny."

"Hmm." He looks forbidding. He's just made me come three times and told me that's it until he gets back. I'm really hoping he'll relent and let me come over the phone for him.

"I need a play friend," I say, absently. "A slave sister, to love when you're not here."

"That would be nice," he says, and smiles. "That would be very nice indeed."

Michael dressed me oddly for an evening at the club. Gone was the usual latex, leather, or lace. The '40s-style dress hugged my torso and flared to my knee. Its soft, clingy brown material was dotted with tiny rose buds. A demure outfit, except for the way my breasts pushed out of the bodice, for the height of the heel on my red, red shoes.

They were high enough to make me clutch onto his arm as he walked me to a back room at the club. Inside, several naked men and women knelt along the wall. He passed by the first few, bringing me to a stop in front of a curvy young woman with long, light brown hair. I knew her vaguely, Liz Massey. She'd lived with her dom, but he'd died of cancer just over a year ago. It was a really sad story. She still wore a collar around her neck, a leather strip with a stone of some sort in it. Other than that, she was naked, shining hair plaited and a little patch of fur on her mons. Michael hunkered down in front of her and raised her chin, peering solicitously into her eyes, that stance I knew so well. I watched as her lips parted, and she looked at him wide eyed. He looked up at me and took my hand, drawing me in closer.

"What do you think, Saph? Would you like her?"

"Is she for me?" My voice sounded awed, incredulous. I was the little girl at the pound.

"Sure, she's for you. What do you think?"

I looked at the woman on the floor. Her breasts were full and pillowy, large nipples rosy against her smooth skin. Her hips and stomach were sweetly curved, and the hands that lay on her thighs looked more capable than elegant. Her nails were short and neat. She was beautiful.

"Oh, Michael, she's perfect! Can we take her home?"

Michael stood and held out his hand to Liz, who took it and rose to her feet.

At home, I hung up the coat she'd traveled from the club in, and she was naked again. Michael fed her sips of water and led her to the playroom, up onto the table padded in dark leather. He positioned her on hands and knees, her braid hanging over one shoulder. I sat on my cushion and watched, with eager breath. Michael ran his fingers down her spine, navigating each vertebra, passing so gently into the cleft between her buttocks and feeling of the plump flesh beyond. Liz's body undulated as he cupped her sex, pressed up with the heel of his hand. I could see her eyebrows knit with the effort of staying silent. Michael pushed her back into position with one finger between her shoulder blades and walked around in front of her. He stroked her full lips, then raised her head with light pressure under her chin. I could feel his fingertips on my own skin, his effortless instruction, and I knelt up straighter.

"Such a pretty kitten," he said, grasping the braid at the nape of her neck and pressing her mouth to the ridge of his erection. "I am so looking forward to seeing what you can do."

I worried that Liz's eyes were looking suspiciously shiny, but she closed them when Michael walked back to the other end of the table. With one hand on the small of her back, he started to smack the undercurve of her buttocks with rhythmic, gentle blows, working his way from the outer edge to her inner thigh. Liz gasped and writhed, and Michael reached up a lazy hand and twined it in her hair to hold her in position. He switched his attention to her pussy, swinging his hand up in between her spread thighs over and over, pulling her head back. Beneath her soft, open-mouthed moans, I could hear the noise of his smacks change as she got wetter.

But the tenor of Liz's cries were changing too. Before I could whisper "Sir," Michael saw that Liz was communicating a different kind of pain. He stopped and stroked her back, gentled her. She knelt there, hunched over, and sobbed, wrapping her arms around herself, emitting hoarse, panicked cries. Michael put his arms around her, but that made it worse. A tilt of his head and I ran over to cradle the naked, shaking woman, drew her to me and held her until her shivering sobs abated. Michael put a blanket around her and lifted her from the table. He brought her to sit between us on the huge floor cushion. When she was settled against me, he stroked her hair from her face and gently ran a finger along the collar she wore.

"Do you feel disloyal?"

Liz nodded. "Yes. No. I…guilty, maybe. But, it's the sadness too." Her voice dropped to a whisper. "You remind me…"

"Is this the first time since he died?" She shook her head. Nodded.

"Yes. No. I didn't get this far." Her fingers touched the collar, held it. I had a sudden fear that someone might have tried to take it off. My chest contracted at the thought.

"What did he tell you, Liz? Did he tell you what to do?" Liz drew a ragged breath and leaned in to me, her body pulling away from the words she was trying to get out.

"He told me to find someone else. I'm trying. I'm trying. I'm lonely, but..." She looked up at him, her blue eyes spilling tears. "I'm lonely for him."

"Of course, darling." Michael wiped them away, raising his eyebrows at me over her head. Oh no. My heart fell. I took his hand, pulling him to the other side of the room for a whispered conversation. Liz looked too broken and exhausted to care that she was being discussed.

"Saphy, she's not ready for this. It's not going to work, I'm sorry."

"Oh, please don't send her back! I know she needs time, but I think we can make her happy again! She wants to try, or she wouldn't be here. I don't want anyone else, Sir, I want Liz, I want to help her. I can work on this, I have a good feeling. We just need to be patient. Let me bring her to bed with me and look after her, please, don't send her home all by herself." I made shameless baby eyes, hoping this was a day when they'd work.

Michael relented.

"Okay, Saph. This was not what I had in mind for us, but I'll play it your way a little while and see." He kissed my forehead and let me put Liz to bed.

If I'd had doubts, they dissolved as soon as I slipped under the covers with the warm, curvy woman. She was racked with tiredness and pain, and she rested her head on my chest and let me stroke her. I kneaded her shoulders and tested her soft skin, running my hands over her until she softened under my touch and met my gentle kisses with her own. I pressed her nipples to hard beads, kissed her wrists, and licked the silk of her inner elbow until she mewed and pressed herself against me. Then I started to explore her pussy, checking for wetness and finding her still hot and swollen, juice coating my questioning fingers as soon as I opened her up. I spread her meltwater onto her nipples, circling it around and around the way people coax music from the rim of a wineglass, then I bent my head to her breasts and licked her clean as I pressed my fingers into her sweet, tight little cunt. This time, she didn't cry. I could feel how there was no trigger for her grief without Michael there to fill the empty man-space Liz ached for so keenly. She was ready; she just had to be brave.

"It's okay, Liz, you can have this. Don't be scared," I whispered into her ear. I bit down on her nipple, working her hard and pressing my thumb over her clit. "Let it go for me, darling. Show me what you can do."

She was elemental. I had never seen an orgasm like the one she had in my bed, on my hand, that night. Her pussy sucked at my fingers with hunger, and she was so hot I felt my hand would burn. The orgasm wrenched from deep inside her, pulled me in, and I could feel myself spasming just from witnessing her throes. I wished Michael had been there to see the depths of her passion and her response. Afterward she was wrung out, speechless, and she fell asleep cleaved to me. Later in the night, Michael joined us, crossing the room softly, and slipping in behind me, and we slept, three together. I wondered how possessive the arm he wound around me was.

The next morning found Liz sweet and mellow. A little of the weight seemed to have lifted from her shoulders. I brought her down to the dining room and fed her bits of fruit from a bowl, sips of tea. Michael came in to taste the mango on my lips and whisper that he had something for me to try on. Liz watched his teasing from behind lowered lashes, bowing her head for his kiss and breathing a morning greeting. My heart clenched. I wanted her here with us.

In the playroom, Michael led me to the mirror and slipped off my robe. I stepped out of the puddle of silk at my feet and into the gleaming black knee boots he proffered. Michael laughed and spun me round slowly in a circle, one hand above my head.

"Oh, Saphina."

Next came a black leather corset that he laced effortlessly but still left me a little breathless. It held me like another skin. Last was a tinier-than-tiny thong that tied with little black silk bows. He sighed.

"It's a good thing I like to share you, Saphina." He stood behind me, rested one hand on my belly and slid the other one over the slip of silk that covered my mound. "I hope I see something good this morning." He pinched my thigh as he let me go.

"Yes, Sir." My heart was in my mouth. And thumping between my legs as well, it seemed.

I walked back to Liz, getting the feel of the new stride the heels necessitated. There was no hesitating in boots like those. They turned me into someone else. I had a clever master. He had bound me into a completely new role. I could feel his warm palm where it had settled over my pubis, owning me. Liz was clearing the table when I entered the dining room. She turned and her mouth fell open at the sight of me.

"What do you think, kitten? Could you be ready?" She nodded, dumbfounded. I waited.

"Oh! I..."

"Yes?"

"I mean, yes, Ma'am. I want to be ready." I leaned over her, taller in my heels, and she pressed a feather-light kiss to the

bare curve of my breast where it pushed out of the corset. "Yes,
Ma'am." It was a whisper. I took a length of black silk ribbon
from the drawer and tied it around her neck, hiding the collar.

"We know it's there, but we can't see it, just for the moment.
How's that?" She touched the bow, an involuntary gesture,
feeling the collar beneath for a second. She nodded. I pushed the
robe off her shoulders, then turned heel and marched into the
playroom, relieved when I heard her quiet footfalls behind me.

Michael reclined on the couch, reading. I peeped at the book
in his hands—he really was reading it—such a sanguine man.
My heart was in my throat, and he was engrossed in a thriller.

"Say good morning, Liz."

"Good morning, Sir." Her voice was low and sweet, and I
could hear the nerves in it. But nerves only, no loss of control. I
snapped my fingers and she knelt beside me. I stroked her hair.

"Show Sir your breasts, kitten, lift them up for him." She
quickly obeyed, lifting her tits and pushing them together,
weighing their heaviness in her hands. I snatched a crop from the
table and tapped it on her thigh so she would spread them wider.

"Fingers in, Liz, three. Open yourself up." She arched her
back and opened her pussy, fingers sliding in easily, I was happy
to see. Michael put the book down, quietly, on the arm of the
couch. Liz arched her back when I touched the base of her spine,
ran the crop up her side, under the curve of her breast. Her
nipples stood out hard and dark when I ran the tip of the crop
over them. When I tapped and snapped and petted one with it,
she moaned.

"Quiet, kitten, now. I think that Sir might like what he
sees." I pressed her onto hands and knees, a push of my boot
against her pubis made her crawl forward, breasts swaying for
Michael's entertainment. She stopped in front of him, and he
leaned forward, waiting. I held my breath as she put her lips to

his hand. He moved her hair out of her face, and she nuzzled into his palm, kissed the pad of his thumb. I took her by the hair and unzipped Michael's trousers with my right hand. I eased his cock out of his trousers, stroked it, ran the tip against Liz's parted lips. He took my hair and kissed me as I forced Liz onto him in turn, moving her head forward and back and setting a pace for her to suck him. I broke Sir's kiss and moved around behind her, still guiding her head, but running my fingers down her spine, rubbing her buttocks, landing a smack here and there. She was working hard to suck him and thrust her ass back into my hand with each spank. Her legs were splayed wide, her pussy was wet when I eased two fingers in and started to fuck her. Ah, our kitten was happy to be used.

She started making noises, and I could see from Sir's face that they were vibrating through him. I pressed up on her G-spot.

"Don't think about coming yet, little kitten, not till you're told. You'll know when you can. Be a good girl for us, wait now." I pressed harder, letting go of her hair and dropping my other hand to her clit. Liz's hips started to pump in abandon, and she uttered a pleading groan around Michael's cock.

"Alright, kitten, show me." He thrust into her mouth, thumbs on her jaw, and I gave her clit what she needed. I thought her orgasm from the night before had been a once-off, a display of pent-up longing, but the intensity was the same. Her scream was muffled by the length of Michael's cock. He pumped into her, a look of astonishment on his face. It was hard to watch Liz coming and not join in. I hid a smile. Michael had slumped forward over Liz, hand in her hair as she rested on his lap. I raised her head.

"Back to work, Liz, clean him all up with your little cat tongue." I patted her ass, happily. Everything was coming up rosy.

* * *

Michael's plane leaves in three hours. I am on all fours on the
bed, with my legs locked wide apart. It is Sir's hand that guides
our kitten's face to my waiting slit, lets her kiss the silky skin
there before pressing her mouth higher, to the smooth, waiting
rose of my asshole. I whimper when I feel her soft lips there, feel
her tongue flicker and circle. Sir's hand chastises me; his fingers
tweak my clamped nipple. I want to escape, but at the same
time I groan when her questing tongue is taken away. It's soon
replaced with cool lube, rubbed into me by Liz's little fingers.
They gently push and press and rub until two are inside me
and I'm crying into the pillow, hungry for more. More comes.
Her hands spread my cheeks wide, and I feel the different touch
of Sir's cock against me, stroking, nudging—Liz is holding me
open for him, I realize with a groan. I'm so eager for it, Sir's
cock pushes steadily in without much resistance. It hurts, until
I feel soft fingers against my clit, slipping inside me, rubbing
against the wall of my vagina and stroking our master through
the barrier of my skin. I hear his sigh, know he's as affected by
that as I am.

A smack rings out, and then Liz is under me. Her mouth
fastens to my clit, and she licks me just like I taught her. Her
mound is right under my face, a plump cushion, and her clit
is standing out for me to suck on. One of Sir's hands grips my
hips, the other presses an imprisoned nipple, I am filled by him
and by Liz's fingers, surrounded by the scent of her, the noise
of the fucking, our sighs and moans and our flesh meeting. I
am consumed with us. I clench on Sir with all I have, bite at
the kitten clit between my lips, suck it and grind on her face at
the same time. Six more hard, staccato thrusts, and Sir starts
to come inside me, and the electricity zips from him to me. As
I start to contract and scream, squeezing Sir's cock and Liz's

fingers, it passes to her. We all come together until we collapse in a sweaty heap.

I know Michael is checking his watch when he moves away, but he returns with a box. He uncuffs my legs, pats my face where it lies on Liz's lap, and laughs. He leaves us there and goes to shower. When he returns, he's in his suit, immaculate again. No sign he was deep in my ass just minutes before.

"Sit up, girls, I have something for you."

In the box lie two beaten silver anklets, one with a blue gemstone, one with a piece of tiger eye embedded in it. Michael puts the box down and pulls our legs onto his lap, strokes each ankle.

"What do you think? One each? I can even lock them together." He smiles. Each one fastens with a delicate silver lock. The keys are tiny, miniature in his hands. Liz's eyes shine. She holds my hand. He reaches up and touches her collar, still fastened around her neck.

"I've told you before. This stays on you until the day you find yourself taking it off without even noticing. We have plenty of time. And in the meantime—" He places the silver band around her ankle, the other around mine. "In the meantime, there is this."

Liz touches the silver at my ankle, and I run my hand over hers. We watch as he adjusts his tie in the mirror, turns to kiss us good-bye.

"Good-bye, kittens. Be good while I'm gone."

I'll miss him, I always do. But now I have my slave sister, our kitten to care for, until he comes back to us again.

A BEAUTIFUL CORPSE

Craig Sorensen

I sometimes wonder if I'd even be able to get out of bed without you. What, with my lower back the way it is. After a night's sleep, it might as well be a rusted ball joint, for all its flexibility. I wish everything was so stiff.

And what about you, getting down the stairs with that knee that only bends twenty percent of what it originally did?

No, you pulling me up to position, and my bracing you down the stairs, well, it's just a part of our day.

We never talked about it, but I came to realize you bought into the idea "Live fast, die young, leave a beautiful corpse" as much as I did. And what a beautiful corpse you would have left. Oh, that day we met. You seemed so sweet and innocent, your skin was white as a dove, your eyes blue as an early spring sky, your hair red as a five-alarm fire.

Heads turned to you like to a meteor falling to earth. Not the least of which was mine. So glad I was the earth you fell to. Yes, you could have left a beautiful corpse and would have. It wasn't for lack of trying.

Remember the way we used to drink? Hand over fist, tequila to scotch and then whiskey to wash down some ludes. Remember the Sinsemilla to sweeten a line of cocaine?

We took challenges by the balls, didn't we, Michelle? Those cliffs we climbed, including the one that fucked up that beautiful knee, now pocked with scars where they tried to fix it. Things were different back then.

Those nude high-dives to crystal-clear water out at that quarry, especially the one that fucked up my back. My arm from when we were on that new KZ-900 and I lost it. I braced out to absorb the shock, denying you of your corpse aspirations. Now that arm is so fucked up it was easier just to learn to be left-handed.

Your face is wrinkled, feels like a seasoned barnstormer's leather jacket. You're kind of brick-orange from years of sun. Your freckles simply united like small villages swallowed by urban sprawl. Your hair is whiter than your skin once was. Your muscles, sinewy, your breasts were once small and perky, now they're small and pendulous. As you lean over to leverage me, your robe opens to give me a peek. I feel a strange, wonderful twinge. Your nipples still have that rich color, and they're big and plump as ripe black cherries when you're stimulated. Did you hear them? I did. They're begging to be sucked. You try to pull your robe over that nipple, and I grab your hand.

Remember how I used to hold your hands over your head and have my way with your sensitive tits until you positively had to be fucked. Lord how you could beg. Just the need in your eyes was enough, but the way your voice got in on the act didn't hurt. Oh, your sigh when I opened my pants and let it fall free but denied you, and you unable to act, bound by four of my best silk ties to the corners of the oversized bed. That bed used to fucking groan like it would buckle at your command. We did collapse a bed or two or three, didn't we?

Your eyes are still that powerful blue, still so vibrant and alive after all these years. "Get the hell up, Lars." You try to tug my left hand from holding your robe open. "Got things to do today."

"You know better." We both know we don't have shit to do today. And what if we did? We couldn't do most of them.

No, like you, my muscles will do what they can, but the structure underneath just doesn't work right anymore, and I don't have it left in me to fight with them. So we get up and pretend. Team up and make his-and-hers bowls of oatmeal with our three good arms, three good legs, and our one good back.

"Get up, you old buzzard." You tug again.

I wink.

You tilt your head and give me that funny grin, your teeth like the picket fence in front of our tumbledown cottage. Your full cracked lips are like a pink road with potholes. Amazing how very soft they still feel when we kiss. I love how we kiss a lot to this day, but fucking? Well, remember how we used to fuck? There wasn't a place we didn't fuck. If we had one of those CSI things that picked up the hint of sex juices, maybe made things glow green, our house would glow like a golf course in spring midday sun. Doggie-style, standing face to face, you lifted against the wall, me holding you like a wheelbarrow, you on top pinning my elbows pumping me, you sideways taking me upside down with a twist, my hand leveraging against your beautiful throat. Feeling the hoarseness in your moans like an old phone receiver in my hand.

Bound and down, fucking in a car, in a bar, up a tree, in the sea. Forgive me if I got my Seuss all over you, but sometimes it seems that's all I have left.

We once joked that the *Kama Sutra* was for sissies, then I ripped your panties off, bent you backward over the neighbor's coffee table while they made Tequila Sunrises in the kitchen, your hips arched unnaturally and my cock squeezed downward in your magnificent cunt. Damn I was hard that night. I pulled out, hauled you home, and turned you over my thigh and spanked you cardinal red for making me miss out on that cold drink. Those two were stiffs, but man they could mix a drink. Wonder what ever happened to them? Anyway, I carted you upstairs over my shoulder, strapped you down to the bed like a fresh drum skin on a big conga. Tight. So fucking tight as I curled into your splayed body. Oh, the rhythms I pounded out that night. Oh, the melodies your voice composed. Call and response, that's what they say. It's been years since we fucked like that. How long has it been since we fucked at all, my sweet Michelle?

They say it's what's on the inside that counts, but on the outside you're beautiful like the moon, marked by a lifetime taking unfiltered meteors, refusing to fall from the sky.

I feel it. A strange sensation. A strange, wonderful sensation: My dick feels so heavy. I tug your arm. You curse at me as you try to steady. Bet you forgot how strong my good arm is. I laugh kind of mean and tug harder. You make me pay the price. You land on me like a jumper from the twelfth floor into a stuntman bag. It hurts like fucking hell. I grunt.

"Serves you right." You laugh like when you used to get me all turned on and ran off after I stripped. Make me chase you so you could watch my burgundy hard-on bounce. I was faster than you, but man you could cut a corner. When I finally caught up, I'd put all my weight down, trap your ankles under my shoulders. Gather your body in mine and compress you like a Ferrari in one of those car-crusher-things. Fuck, you used laugh and taunt me when I got like that.

Now your weight is centered on that bad spot in my spine. It hurts, and I keep getting harder. Your right tit landed conveniently close to my mouth. What kind of gentleman would I be if I didn't oblige? Okay, I'm no gentleman, but still I fumble to one-hand your robe, and you open wide. I draw one nipple in my mouth.

What a beautiful sight. I move from breast to breast, tongue and teeth, and I'm thankful for all those dentists' appointments along the way. I still have them in some fashion. I bite. "More." I bite harder. "Yeah, that's it."

Your pussy feels so fucking good on my thigh. I need to get in.

But the logistics just aren't that simple anymore, Michelle. We're bound by limitations. I keep my back tilted just so, you extend that bad knee at a bearable angle like a bow ready to sling an arrow as you position.

Your hot old cunt engulfs me. Oh, that feels so great. I yank those magnificent tits like handles. We manage the trajectory like Houdini getting out of a big box full of water.

Water. You're wet as that river we swam in and nearly got washed out in class-four rapids. Our hearts still pounding double time, mouths still awash with adrenaline, we only got back to the shore by teaming up. That was after I fucked up my arm, and you saved my life, kept me from my aspirations. Remember that big rock we fucked on while still feeling the electric charge and tasting the adrenaline of cheating that "beautiful corpse god" again? That old rock afforded only one position we could manage. Funny, but as I recall, it was something like this moment. It's like being bound by that rock's shape this many years later. And why not? That was one epic fuck.

My cock is completely hard. Don't know the last time it did that. Feels wonderful. You slide along it like a master ballerina. Tip kissed by your pussy lips, then gulped all the way up you.

You haven't lost a move. On your good arms, you sway that perfect rhythm. Musicians call it muscle memory. I call it heaven to be in you again. I could die like this. Oh, you're slick and smooth. It really is what's on the inside that counts, my sweets.

Ha!

Know what, Michelle? I'm a bit numb down there, have been since the back injury, but I feel you now. I feel you in ways I never felt you before. Maybe the weird way my back is tilted is giving me more sensation like a hose suddenly unkinked, a rush of urgent water. Maybe it's all in my head. Either way, you sway on me like a weeping willow in the wind. Now I shift my back, to try to kink a measure of that numbness. I don't want this to end.

Your good knee locks up. Your bad one must hurt like fire. I know my back does, so I pump hard into you, and you meet every thrust.

Are your grunts pain or pleasure? Mine are both, thankfully.

Pain. Damn, you could administer a spanking, Michelle. My strong hips draped over you, my pants pulled down to my ankles and my hard cock rubbed raw by the seam of your blue-jean thighs, a hair brush cracking over one cheek then the other until I throbbed, then you turned me over, pinned my elbows under your curled legs, grabbed fistfuls of my long, curly hair, and made me eat you for a half-hour, only releasing me when convinced I'd given your pussy sufficient attention. Then you grabbed my hair again and made me eat some more.

I haven't eaten so good in years.

By god, I'm still hard. I take every forceful drive of your pussy. Viagra is for sissies. I work your clit, surrounded in white-cloud pubic hair, with my left hand and watch your face open like a kid ripping into the best Christmas gift ever. Your orgasmic shout harkens back fifty years. It's like the song of the furies: irresistible. Crash me on your shore. My nuts squeeze tight to my crotch like a new peach emerged from an old, knurled branch.

I hold my breath as I sputter into you. I continue to hold to feel this orgasm more intensely, but I have to gasp a breath before I fucking pass out. I see you. I see stars. I pull air.

Perfect, Michelle. Perfect.

You collapse to my chest. I feel the fast pounding your heart. I wrap my good arm, then my lousy one, around you and hold you tight to savor. I time my breaths with the rise and fall of your chest. Your nipples poke like fingers. Your low voice emanates from your chest with each exhale as we fight to get our pulses back down. Your skin is so perfect, rough and soft all at once.

You kiss my cheek. Those perfect lips.

We lived fast, but didn't die young. I can't speak for mine, but when your body finally is a corpse, it'll be more beautiful than it was at sixty, or fifty, or forty. That much I know.

I grunt. "Ow, my fucking back." It spasms as you shift your body.

"You love it, and you fucking know it." You grab my face and wink.

"Almost much as you. Christ, help me up."

You rise off me like girly-girl push-ups, swing your good leg over, and fight to a standing position. You work your knee as best as you can, then take my left arm, and we manage to get me upright. I fold my left arm around your waist and you brace. You reach for your discarded robe, but I hold you fast. I don't want you to dress. "Leave it, Michelle."

Yes, you are so gorgeous. More gorgeous than you were at thirty, or even fucking twenty. You are perfect.

I nestle my nose in your ear, my cock still wet with you. "You still fuck perfect. Let's make a big breakfast, just like this, you

beautiful bitch. Remember? Hot bacon splatters feel as delicious as they taste."

You slap my naked butt nice and hard. I felt that sting but good! You laugh. "You still got it, you handsome bastard."

That I do. I got what counts: you. I pull you a bit tighter to my hip and we work toward the stairs.

EINE KLEIN SPANKING

Clarice Clique

Rozalyn was wearing nothing but her favorite red thigh-high boots. I stared with raw desire at her beautiful ebony skin and the delicious curves of her naked ass and breasts as she walked about the room taking her time choosing between a whip and a cat-o'-nine-tails. My own movement was restricted by how tightly she'd tied me to her four-poster bed, and although I'd never admit it to her, the sheer size of the dildos she'd pushed into my pussy and ass. Sometimes she teased me by moving out of my line of vision and noisily playing with herself, but right now she was leaning against the wall stroking the tip of a whip with her long fingernails. Every single thought in my head should have been focused on my gorgeous friend and what she was about to do to me. So why could all my years of obedience training not keep my mouth closed?

"He's so hot, Rozalyn, I mean really really seriously hot. And did I mention he's German? The scene over there's supposed to be wild, isn't it? I've never been, I meant to, but other things have always got in the way, but now a German guy is right next door to me, that's got to be fate, hasn't it? Imagine him barking out orders in that harsh accent, and they're supposed to be such a disciplined and efficient country, aren't they? I'd be sure to do things wrong and need lots of punishment."

"You don't have to be German to want to punish you, Audrey." Rozalyn came over to the side of the bed and looked down at me. "I'm ordering you to go 'round and talk to him. He's your new neighbor for fuck's sake, how hard is it to make up an excuse to say hello? Introduce yourself, take around a welcome basket of homemade cupcakes, ask to borrow a cup of sugar, I don't care. Just do it, or I'll do things to you that not even you with your filthy little mind could imagine."

"Yes. You're right. But do you think a welcome basket would be too much? I mean, he moved in two weeks ago, is it too late to welcome him? Are cupcakes a good idea? Maybe too homely, not giving off the right signals, what about cookies, are they better, everyone loves cookies, right?"

"Cookies are great. They tell a man very clearly that you want him to bend you over and fuck you harder than you've ever been fucked in your life. Now enough with the talk, you're not normally this annoying."

Rozalyn opened a drawer of her side table and pulled out a ball gag.

"I'll be good, you don't have to use that, you know I'm not the biggest fan of being gagged."

"That's kind of the point of a punishment. If you listened to yourself you'd know you deserve a lot worse." She momentarily put the whip down and fastened the gag around my mouth and smiled down at me. "Now we can start having fun."

She picked the whip up and brought it down on my tits so hard that her own breasts swayed with the effort. Rozalyn was right, the fun was starting, but still I did something I'd never done before. I closed my eyes and imagined it was someone else punishing me; a tall, muscled German man with a stern accent whipping his new American slut.

So, this was the first meeting with my dream master-to-be:

He answered the door almost immediately after I knocked, like he'd known I'd been pacing up and down my kitchen for the last hour and he was just waiting for me to work up the courage to come see him. A good sign.

"Hi, I'm your neighbor. Sorry it's taken me so long to come over and introduce myself but you know how it is busy, busy, busy. I made you some cookies. And cupcakes. And muffins of the blueberry, chocolate chip, and apricot variety. Hope you like something in there."

I held the basket out to him. He stared at it for a moment before taking it.

"Thank you," he said in that beautiful thick, hard accent.

"My name's Audrey. Like the film star. Audrey Hepburn."

He nodded. "You look something like her."

I beamed and glowed even though I'd heard that compliment a hundred times before and much more eloquently put; yet with him it didn't sound like an empty compliment but a statement of fact, and that turned me on.

"What's your name?" I asked.

"Wolfgang, like the composer, Wolfgang Amadeus Mozart."

"Wolfgang?" I pronounced it in an English way, as in a gang of canine predators, and for some stupid reason I couldn't stop laughing. A bad sign.

"What is funny?" he said in all seriousness.

"Nothing," I said through the giggles I couldn't control. "Nothing at all. I better get home. Hope you like the cakes.

Bring the basket back whenever. Bye."

I carried on laughing until I was in my kitchen with my back to the door, then I sunk to the floor and wondered what idiotic part of me had been in control in creating that essential first impression.

So that was our first meeting, and for ten minutes I thought it would be our last and was considering whether moving to Alaska would be a viable option and if that would be far enough away. Then there was a knock at my door, and there he was in all his six-foot-five glory standing on my porch.

"I am returning your basket," he said holding it out for me. "Thank you for the food. Would you like to come to dinner with me on Tuesday evening?"

"Yes," I said, silently thanking the god who'd created a man who was attracted to women who laughed at his name. "Yes, I'd love to go to dinner with you."

Before Tuesday I'd tried on at least a hundred different outfits and played with my vibrator almost as many times.

After Tuesday I'd gained a boyfriend called Wolfie and learned that Wolfie had had five lovers, all of them long term, none of them that interested in sex, only one of his girlfriends had given him a blowjob. This information obviously made me despair for the women of Germany letting such a piece of man go to sexual waste, unless all men looked like him in Germany, in which case nothing would stop me visiting that country again.

We fell into a routine of seeing each other two evenings during the week and one day of the weekend. This suited me fine, as it created lots of space for allure and anticipation; smiling across at each other when we left for work in the morning, bumping into each other by accident in the street, watching him work in his garden, all the time knowing we had a date set when we'd be together.

What was more problematic and outside of my experiences was the way he was with me. It was probably my fault for getting carried away with cultural stereotypes, but it was kind of a shock to be given a fluffy pink teddy bear that was bigger than I was. I thought for a while he wanted me to play at being the sweet little girl corrupted by the big bad older man, but what corrupter spends three weeks of dates doing nothing more risqué than pecking his girl on the lips?

In the end my lust beat my patience down, and I gave up waiting to be seduced. My first encounters were usually passion-fuelled, clothes-ripping affairs that happened in alleyways, on staircases, in toilets, leaving my body raw and bruised. With my new German boyfriend I took his hand and led him upstairs to my bedroom, moved the big pink teddy off the bed, and we lay down together fully clothed and faced each other. I put my arms around him, and we kissed, gentle loving kisses. My hands slid down the back of his jeans, I pressed my tongue between his lips, and as he responded I moved my hand around to the front and began to slowly wank him. He moaned and rolled onto his back; I undid his belt and pulled his pants down. His cock was even larger than I'd imagined. I didn't attempt to deep throat it, instead sucking and licking the head while one of my hands squeezed his balls. My other hand pulled up my skirt, and I rubbed my thumb over my clit. I was happy tasting him, breathing in the scent of his sex, and waiting for the moment when his confidence and desire grew and he'd put his hands on the back of my head and pushed me down onto the full length of his cock.

That didn't happen.

He stroked my hair gently until the moment his body shuddered and he let out an enormous groan as he shot into my mouth. Then he pulled me up to him and kissed me with the scent of his spunk still lingering on my lips.

"Would you like me to lick you out?" His accent sounded almost mechanical, and the only answer I could make was laughter.

I laughed so much that we didn't have intercourse but fell innocently asleep in each other's arms.

The next morning I rectified this by mounting his early morning erection. He woke up with me grinding on top of him, orgasms pulsing through me as I used his cock for my own pleasure. Immediately his hips bucked up into mine, like a reflex, and his own orgasm was much louder and more violent than any of mine.

"Thank you," he said.

I smiled down at him and caressed his sensitive body with my lightest touch. I could be patient. He was worth it.

His lack of experience made him so easy to please. He made me feel like I was the most amazing woman in the world when I swallowed his spunk or finally convinced him I liked it when he came over my face. Young men had never held any attraction for me, but Wolfgang's face when I oiled my breasts and rubbed his cock between them made me think of a teenage boy experiencing the first joys of illicit masturbation. There was a certain pleasure to this; things I must have done hundreds of time gained a new adventurous quality when I did them with him. Having sex with my German in a secluded field in the middle of nowhere gave the same thrills and sense of exhibitionism as when I'd sucked and ridden three men one after another in the back of a taxicab in central London. But there was a big drawback. An enormous drawback.

The more my life became mingled with my handsome neighbor's, the more I thought about what I was missing. It surprised
me how easily I fell into a monogamous relationship, and sometimes I could convince myself that I wasn't missing the sex life I'd
previously enjoyed. But as the days, weeks, and months passed,
the yearning only got stronger. It'd always been a part of my
adult life; it had been part of my very initiation into becoming
an adult.

Not many of my friends believed I'd remained a virgin until
I was twenty-two, but it was true. There'd been no need to
rush into having intercourse, as I'd already found sexual pleasures elsewhere: a married man who balanced his conscience
by never kissing or having sex with me but who spanked me
relentlessly. And that experience had just been the beginning.
As I grew older I met other men and women, sometimes by
accident, sometimes on purpose, who pushed and pulled my
sexuality so far that I was left uncertain what my limits were,
and even whether I had any.

And now I was settling down with a man who made me smile
more than anyone else ever had, a man who said his greatest
sexual moment was when I rode him that first time. I tried
searching for his darker fantasies, hoping they would mirror
mine, but whenever spanking was mentioned he responded with
some variation of:

"I can't see what is fun about that. How is it nice to hurt
someone?"

I tried to turn him on with what I considered to be milder
stories from my past, stroking his cock as I whispered into his
ear. I told him of the time I spent most of a weekend bound hands
to feet and blindfolded with people (I had no idea whether they
were friends or strangers) taking turns to spank me. His prick
would respond and stiffen under my touch, but I would always

say too much, telling him how raw my body felt, how even the soft fabric of clothes against my skin would sting and remind me of the punishment I'd taken.

Finally, after more nagging and teasing and persuading and promises than you'd believe, I convinced him to at least try it out.

I wore a black bra under a white shirt, over-the-knee socks, and a short pleated skirt with no knickers to complete the look. Nothing too hardcore, no PVC, no bondage, and the only leather was on my shoes. I opened the door to him in character, giggling and teasing but backing away when he tried to kiss me. I knocked a pen onto the floor and bent over in front of him to pick it up, giving him a full view of my naked rump. He put his hands on my hips, but I wriggled away and made him chase me, letting him catch me long enough for me to rub my ass against the growing bulge in his trousers before I twisted out of his embrace and ran away again. It took a lot of willpower not to drop to my knees and suck on his cock, but I'd worked so hard for this moment, I couldn't let it pass so easily.

"I'm a very very naughty girl," I said. "You need to punish me. You need to spank me."

It was difficult to play at being a coy little cockteaser when I had to push my big muscled man down onto a chair and position myself over his lap, but I think I just about pulled it off.

I imagined his excitement at having my body in his power, at looking down and seeing the curves of my ass and knowing he could leave the red imprint of his hand on my naked skin. I could feel the barely contained aggression of his prick pressing against me, desperate to pound into me. But when his hand struck me it was more like a friendly pat I would expect from a drunken uncle, not from a passion-filled lover.

"I'm a wicked girl," I said trying not to sound disappointed.

"Maybe you need to punish me a bit harder to make me into a good girl."

He patted my ass again; it might have been a bit harder but it was a very close call.

"I've been really really bad, really really really bad. Punish me."

He sighed and gently lifted me off his lap. "I'm sorry, Audrey, you know how much I love you, how I want to do anything and everything to please you, but this isn't working, is it?"

I managed to give him a small smile. "Perhaps you'd prefer breast bondage? I thought that might be a bit difficult to start with, but lots of men I know go mad for it."

I looked at the expression on his face and did what I probably should have done from the start, dropped to my knees and released his erection from his jeans. I let all the words disappear and instead filled my mouth with his prick.

I'd only gone to see Rozalyn to catch up on a bit of a gossip, maybe to ask some advice; I wasn't sure how I ended up naked in her basement with my back curved over a barrel and my hands and feet bound to metal hooks in the floor. Although it might have been triggered when after about five minutes of listening to me she said, "Enough whining, slut, take your clothes off and go to my dungeon."

Rozalyn had been wearing your average office clothes when I arrived, but now she was clad in a black PVC cat suit that covered all of her body and head with holes for her eyes, mouth, breasts, and cunt. She leaned over me, making her dark nipples caress my pink ones. My body tensed as I knew what would be coming next, whenever she kissed or stroked my breasts it was always the prelude to the same thing: big heavy iron pegs clamped all over my chest.

And that was what she did now, pinching them onto my skin faster than normal so I could barely breathe between each gasp of pain.

"Rozalyn. I've forgotten the safe word. I've never needed it before. But I think I'm going to need you to take things a bit easier on me. I'm out of practice."

Rozalyn gave a small shake of her head. She put the peg she was holding in her hand onto the side of my breast but did not place any more.

"You'll have to please me in other ways then," she said and stood above my head.

She started by rubbing her clit against my nose, then she pushed her pussy against my mouth. Obediently I thrust my tongue into her and enjoyed the feeling of being enveloped by the heat of her sex. She ground down into me, and I realized how lazy I'd got having a lover who was so easy to please. I worked my mouth hard, pressing back up into her as she pushed down on me. She flicked her nails against the pegs as I tongue-fucked her; when I flicked my tongue over her clit she yanked one off and we both screamed out.

"Now that pleases me," she said.

I concentrated on her clit, grazing it with my teeth and working my tongue over it again and again as she pulled the pegs off my skin until there were just two left on my nipples. She put one hand on each clip, and I pushed my mouth against her, kissing and licking her pussy and waiting for the irresistible pain. In the same instant she wrenched the pegs off and came in a big squirting gush into my open mouth.

We both panted deep heavy breaths for a few minutes before she moved away from me.

"I enjoyed that so much, I think we should do it again."

I smiled and sighed and cried out as she put the pegs back

onto my now more tender skin. Somewhere deep inside me was a voice wondering what my German lover would think if he could see me. I buried the pangs of guilt and focused on the wet pussy that would soon be on my face again.

I lay naked on my bed with my German boyfriend, watching the tears in his eyes that were falling onto my skin as he ran his fingers over the marks on my body. I'd explained what happened with Rozalyn three times now, but with each explanation instead of reassuring him I was making both of us feel worse.

"It's not cheating or being unfaithful, Wolfie, Rozalyn and I are old friends, we play together now and again. It's nothing serious, just sex. Not like me and you at all, nothing to be jealous or upset about."

"Are you a lesbian? Do you get more pleasure being with a woman than with me?" His voice was unusually soft. I strained to hear his words.

"I guess I don't believe in labeling people in that way. There's a quote from Simone de Beauvoir that I found and memorized ages ago when I was a student, 'In itself, homosexuality is as limiting as heterosexuality: the ideal should be to be capable of loving a woman or a man; either, a human being, without feeling fear, restraint, or obligation.' And that kind of influenced me, or it summed up how I felt about relationships. And, oh, I don't know why I'm quoting at you. I know you don't want me to quote at you. I just don't know what to say or do to make this better. I'm not used to feeling like this."

"Do you love me, Audrey? Can you love me as I am?"

He stared into my eyes. I felt like every beat of my heart would be the last.

"I love you. Forgive me and I'll be better. I can change and learn how to be a traditional girlfriend. I love you and I want you more than anything else."

He put his arms around me and pulled me against his chest. "You're vibrant and beautiful and amazing. I don't want you to change for me. Share your experience with me, teach me how to become the lover you desire."

"I do desire you."

"I know. And I know you desire more, so show me this more."

"Would you like to see some of my porn? I've got books and films, it might help you to see the kind of things I do."

He pushed me away from him and again stared into my eyes in that way that made me feel so vulnerable and so alive.

"I want you to show me. I want to experience the things that excite you, I want you to do to me the things you like done to you."

I considered how to explain to him that I was the submissive, that I wanted to have my body forced and tied into the most prone positions, to feel the tip of a whip caressing my skin before it lashed against me, I wanted my nipples clamped, my mouth gagged, I wanted to wake up the next morning to a reflection that was covered with scratches and bruises.

"You've got to obey everything I say without question or hesitation," I said. "And if it gets too much the safe word is Simone, you say that and then I'll stop whatever I'm doing. If you're sure you want to do this, then turn away and let me prepare."

"Thank you," he said and he turned his face into the bed while I walked over to my wardrobe.

I put on a red corset, stockings, and stiletto heels. Carefully I reapplied my makeup, choosing dark sultry colors, hoping that if I could create the right look I could become the right woman. I slowly chose a selection of toys, giving him as much time as possible to change his mind about this thing before it even started. Then I took a deep breath, imagined I was Rozalyn, and turned to my lover.

"I want you on your hands and knees on the floor. Dogs should know better than to get on the furniture. I think you need more training." I bit down on my lip. Was the thing about dogs too much? Was it too early?

But he obeyed me, kneeling on the floor, resting on his elbows, his naked buttocks presented before me. I wished I didn't feel so nervous. Before Wolfgang moved in next door it wasn't an emotion I was familiar with sexually. Sex was about losing all your inhibitions, it was pure id, the most primal, bestial force. It wasn't about pausing in front of the beautiful body of your lover wondering how to proceed. He was willing to do anything I told him, to obey my every command, and instead of arousing me it made me feel weighted with responsibility. I liked the sensation of having all control taken away from me, the liberation of doing nothing except enjoy, but now I needed to think about his feelings. Standing with him prostrate before me, I realized how important it was that this man who'd become entwined in my life could share this part of my world with me.

I looked at the toys I'd selected, but they all looked too severe for my gentle lover. I slowly walked around him, my heels clicked on the floor. It was a sound that had aroused me many times, bound and blindfolded, shivering in anticipation at the knowledge that someone was approaching me. I looked down at my German, and his figure made my breath stop. It seemed unbelievable that one person could be made so flawlessly. His broad shoulders tapering into that narrow waist and the perfect curve of his bottom. And he was all mine. For the first time I experienced a sense of ownership, that at some level this strong man belonged to me, that he had never done this for anyone but me.

I raised my hand and slapped down on the fullest part of his buttocks. He gasped, but I gave him no time to breathe before I brought my hand down for a second and third time. The *thwack* of my skin meeting his filled the room. My sexual side didn't just awaken; it took complete control of my being.

I spanked him five times on each buttock, creating red blushes on his tight cheeks. But it wasn't enough; my inner beast demanded more before it'd be satisfied. I picked up a black riding crop, one that I'd brought years ago with the intention of employing it for its proper use, but it'd found its way into my first lover's hand and had since become one of my favorite pieces of equipment.

With the tip of the crop I lightly traced the clean line of his spine, down from the nape of his neck to the small of his back, then let it rest in the secret valley between his buttocks. I watched his muscles waiting for him to relax, for the tension in his shoulders to be released, before raising the crop and whipping it sharply down on his ass. My pussy was moist, but I contained my passion. I bought the whip down on his skin several more times, watching the marks form on his toned buttocks, and knew I had to stop or I'd whip his whole body. I imagined his strong thighs and back decorated in the same manner as his ass, and it gave me a sensation of both incredible power and humbleness at how much he trusted me.

He was silent as I whipped him. When I took my punishment I liked to scream out, living the full intensity of each stroke. I pictured him staying in this posture, not uttering a sound, as I fulfilled all my dominating fantasies on his passive body. He might be hating every moment, willing it to end, but he would endure it all for me.

"Lie on your back." I thought it was better not to look at the tender skin on his ass any longer in case my willpower failed.

He immediately obeyed.

His cock was fully erect. I wanted to smile and hug him, to tell him how happy I was, but the silence between us was intoxicating.

I sat astride him, facing toward his feet, as I knew if I looked into his face I wouldn't be able to maintain this mistress persona. He slid into me, and I felt immediate pleasure enclosing his whole length with my hungry self. I rode him hard with a new freedom. His fists were clenched on the floor, and the sound of his moans mingled with my own. I could feel the tension in him desperate to be released. Another time I'd tease him, only allowing him to come when I was ready, but today I responded by riding him harder, grinding into his groin until the power of his orgasm shot through us both, making me shiver and cry out with animal passion.

We held each other in a tight embrace, whispering our love in secret words. There were things we said and other things that we didn't need to say.

I was exhausted by all the emotions pounding through my body. The sexual part of me was fighting to regain control, desperate to explore more of this dominant side, to force this large gorgeous man to my will, to use all my toys on him right here and now. But this time I gave control to my calmer side. I knew that our future involved us learning and experimenting, always together. And this knowledge filled me with a warmth and peace I'd never had before.

Later, as we lay in bed, him sleepily spooning me, I bit down on the pillow to stop myself laughing. I was euphorically happy. All I wanted to do was laugh. And fuck. And spank. And whip. And grind. And laugh.

DEFINING
THE TERMS

Sharazade

*W**hether sentence modifiers are a subclass of adverbial is...*
is what? Hotly debated? That's probably stretching it a bit.
Back up a bit, come around another way. *As the largest class of
modifiers, adverbials are...*No. *Modification is essential...*Okay,
not essential, but...Well, actually in one sense, it is essential,
because...But best to pin down the meaning before the usage.
There are x major classes of adverbial modifiers, as follows:...

Midmorning is usually a good time for me to work, but
today I'm blocked. I know what I want to say, so why can't I
just say it? I can feel him waiting for me to be done, too, which
of course just makes me feel more blocked. If he would just leave
the apartment, I could probably work more easily, although I
know better than to say so. Especially since it's his apartment.

He comes up behind me now and lightly caresses my neck
with his fingers. "That looks riveting," he murmurs, though I
can tell that he's looking at me, not the screen. "What are you
working on?"

"Adverbials." I feel his breath now on my neck; it's a distraction, and I wonder if it's meant to be. By now, he knows my weak spots.

"Adverbials." He's lifting my hair out of the way, gently, but with that assured possessiveness that normally melts me. "And what are adverbials good for?"

"Actually, a lot of things." He's not being dismissive, is he? I happen to take my work seriously, thank you very much. I don't bother to explain, though. His hands are now kneading my shoulders, rubbing my upper back.

"This is for that grammar blog?" A kiss to my neck, a definite kiss. "The one you don't have to write?" A hint of teeth now, just grazing the skin. "The one with no deadline?" A bite; not too hard, but firm and with intent. His hands now trace my sides, up and down, a motion I normally love. They pause by my breasts, give an extra squeeze, fingertips playing with my skin through my loosely tied yukata.

"The one that pays me $150 per entry, yes." Of course, at the rate I'm going today, it's not a very good wage, but that's not really the point.

"Hmm. I'm feeling kind of sexy," he says, as if there was any way I could have missed that.

"Well, that's nice for you. Go and feel sexy somewhere else, till I'm done."

His hands freeze in position. He says nothing. A pause, and then abruptly he straightens and walks away. I hope I didn't sound rude, because that wasn't my intention, but I'm a little distracted here. I wouldn't be any good as company, not like this. I know I said that most of today would be for us, but "most" of it is still left, and I'm *working*. (Sort of.)

I can hear him in the next room, picking things up, putting things down, doing something. I'll be extra-sweet to him when

I'm done, I'll make it up to him, I'll get into the mood somehow. But now, back to adverbials.

Suddenly he's behind me, though I hadn't heard him approach. There's a sharp tug on my hair, and my hands fly back instinctively. Immediately my forearms are grabbed; then my hands are pulled behind the chair. I hear the click at the same time I feel metal against my skin. Oh, for...He's handcuffed me. He knows I don't like those things. They look all hot and sexy, sure, but the metal cuts into my skin. "James," I say, trying to keep the irritation out of my voice, "This isn't really—"

He pulls my chair back from the computer and moves to stand in front of me. Tied only at the waist, my yukata has fallen open, and he reaches for my panties, tugging at the sides. I'm surprised to feel him lift me just a bit off the chair and pull the panties down onto my thighs. This is ridiculous. I clamp my knees shut so he can't get them off. He slips a hand between my legs, and we struggle for a bit. My legs are stronger than they look, from all that riding, but he is stronger still, and I lose the struggle—and my underwear. Now I'm thoroughly annoyed.

"James, after lunch, perhaps, I'd be happy to—"

"You know," he says, thoughtfully, "I think I've heard enough out of you." He pulls the tie loose from my yukata. Before I can take in what's happening, he's taken my head in one hand. A squeeze to my jaw has me open my mouth in surprise, and he shoves the panties inside, and then swiftly ties them into place with my yukata sash.

Oh, fuck this! I hate to be gagged, as he well knows, even when I have time for games, which I don't right now. I'm gagged, my hands are in these awful handcuffs, and I'm trying to work. I give a howl of protest, though of course it's muffled by the cloth. I aim a kick at his lower leg—it's all I can reach—but he sees it coming and steps to the side just in time. I try to drive my heel down on his foot, but he dodges that as well. "My, aren't you angry," he says, with just that curl of his upper lip. "This will never do."

He lifts my glasses off my face and places them carefully on the desk. Oh, this does not bode well. From somewhere he picks up a pair of ankle cuffs and Velcros them deftly one to each foot; he crosses my feet at the ankles and clips one cuff to the other. I now can't stand, can't kick...could I lift my arms over the low back of the chair? And then what? I catch a yell in my throat before it can come out (or try to, through the gag) because I'm damned if I'm going to give him the satisfaction.

He pauses for a moment, looking at me, helpless and angry in the chair. If he weren't looking at me so intently, I'd try to slip my hands from the cuffs—I bet my wrists are slim enough to wriggle out, though of course I have no intention of alerting him to this. But his eyes are on me now, and I don't make a move. We are both waiting, considering, watching.

He comes around to the side and, a little awkwardly but with no hesitation, lifts me up off the chair and throws me unceremoniously over his shoulder. I kick and squirm a bit, but where can I go? I don't want him to drop me, because I can't stand up with my feet crossed like this. He carries me, wriggling, over to the bed and tosses me down onto it without any particular care. I lie there, half on my side, half on my back, glaring at him.

"You are my slut, Shar," he says, quietly, deliberately. It isn't phrased as a question, yet he's looking at me as if he expects an answer. I consider for a moment. Pissed off as I am, I am still his. I know this. I nod, ever so slightly. I am not on his side at the moment, but yes, I acknowledge this.

"Well, for one of the world's leading linguists, you seem to have a very poor understanding of what the phrase 'my slut' means, and what it entails," he says, almost patiently. "Allow me then to clarify a few things for you."

Standing over me, he positions me on the bed so that I'm face down, legs stretched down, arms cuffed behind my back. I hear him pick something up and thwack it against his open palm. A solid sound. A paddle? Oh please, not the narrow one, not the one that hurts...but it is, I can tell. I know that sound. Last night I wanted so badly to be paddled, though it didn't happen; but right now, I am filled with dread. Is he angry with me? I've never really been punished by him, not really.

"Let's take it word by word, Shar," he intones, evenly. "'My.' What does 'my' mean? What is 'my'?" I can't answer, of course, gagged as I am, but my mind is racing anyway, as usual. *It's a pronoun, it's a possessive adjective, by function it's a determiner, it's...*As if he could hear my thoughts, here comes his disagreement. *Thwack.* "'My' means that you belong to *me.*" *Thwack.* "James." *Thwack.* "*I* decide what you are going to do." *Thwack!* "Your actions are to please *me.*" *Thwack!* Normally when he hits me, the impacts are interspersed with sweet caresses, but now there is nothing to interrupt the beatings, and they hurt. My ass and thighs are stinging; there is no relief. It's hard to breathe through my nose, and I try to pant though my mouth, but the panties are blocking my breath.

He must have seen me struggling for air, for in one smooth gesture he unties the cloth belt around my head and mouth and pulls the panties out. I gulp a few breaths, sides heaving. I can feel the blood rushing to the surface of my skin; I know it must be flushed and red. "When I want you, what do you say, Shar?" *Thwack!* "Yes, James!" I gasp. "When I tell you to suck my cock, what do you say, Shar?" *Whack!* "Yes, James!" "When I tell you I'm going to fuck you in the ass, what do you say, Shar?" *Whack!* "Yes, James!" Rapid fire, he asks me more questions...

things I hadn't even known he was thinking about, shocking things, but I say yes without hesitation. I know it doesn't matter what he asks me, I will say yes. Almost as if he's realized this at the same instant, he stops. He's panting from the exertion too, and for a few moments we just breathe together, heavily. "Well, Shar," he says, quietly and with no little satisfaction, "you seem to have grasped the concept of 'my' at last." Can a pat to the ass be smug? Oh, yes; yes it can. "Let's move on then to 'slut.'"

He runs his fingertips lightly over my buttocks and back, so lightly I can't even tell if he's touching skin or just the tips of my hairs, but my skin shivers. How I long for a firmer touch!

"What does 'slut' mean, Shar?"

I have no idea if I'm supposed to answer this or not. It's hard for me to gather my thoughts, and putting them into coherent sentences seems an impossible task. But I don't want to be paddled anymore. I can't take more. Before I can sputter something out, he speaks for me.

"A slut isn't someone who just enjoys sex, Shar. A slut needs it. You need it. Your mind may be strong, but your body rules you, darling, your body *is* you, your most fundamental self, and your body craves my touch, and my control. I'm sure if I slipped my hand up between your legs, I'd find you wet."

Oh, how I hope he doesn't test this, because I know he is right....And all the while he's running his hand oh so lightly over my back, my ass, now down my legs...

"You couldn't say no to your desires even if you wanted to," he says. "Allow me to prove it to you."

His hand is heavier now on my body, firm, full contact. Heavenly. The increased blood flow from the paddling has every nerve in my skin singing, and it thirstily drinks up the sensations he provides.

"Look at you react when I touch you, Shar." He squeezes

my inner thigh, just a hint of fingernail, and my body shudders. I can't help it. "Listen to yourself, Shar," he says, dragging a finger down the crack of my ass, and involuntarily I groan with desire. "See how wet you are," and he doesn't even have to touch me, I can feel my juices running down my thighs, but he traces two fingers over my sopping pussy, covers them, and smears the slickness on my ass cheeks.

"I think we understand what 'slut' means now, don't we, Shar?"

"Yes, James," I say, obediently.

"Now all we need to do is put them together. My. Slut. My slut."

As he speaks, I can feel him unclip my ankles from each other and somehow disconnect the chain that holds the handcuffs together, though the metal still encircles each wrist. (*They come apart?* I think through my fog. *I must remember this.*) With one sure motion he turns me over; it's easy now, I'm not fighting anymore. For just a moment he lets me stretch my arms and legs, oh, the ache, then deliberately he takes each arm, pulls it down straight by my side, bends my knees and pushes my ankles up to my ass, and clips the wrist to the ankle, right to right, left to left. It's an open position, comfortable, yet helpless.

"'My slut' means that your body is mine, your desires are controlled by me, you're here for my pleasure," he says as he looks me in the eye. I'm embarrassed to meet his gaze, helpless and dripping like this, but I can't look away.

"You don't need to worry about 'being in the mood,' Shar, because I will put you in the mood when I want you there. As I have." He observes me for a few beats, not speaking; he reaches up and strokes my cheek, my neck, down between my breasts.

"You are mine, and you need me. Don't you, Shar?" he asks.

"Yes, James."

"What do you need?"

I'm not sure how to answer this. "I need you."

"How?" He's moved away from me just a little, not touching me any longer.

I pull at my restraints, trying to touch him, but I can't. "I need you to touch me."

He presses a finger to the top of my knee.

"No, I need more."

Two fingers on my knee. He's being deliberately obtuse, and I hate it.

"*No*, James, touch *me*, touch my thigh," I begin, and he does, a slow, firm stroke down my thigh toward my pussy. Oh heaven. "Kiss me, kiss my thigh," I gasp, and he does. "Bite me," and I feel his teeth, biting every so slowly, inevitably, increasing the pressure till I shiver.

Oh...could it be? Is he really going to give me whatever I ask for? Or is this some further tease, is it a trick? I must try, though....

"Put a finger inside me, James," and yes, he does. "Kiss my pussy, not too hard!" and he does, oh, yes, he does, soft lips pressing down on me, a hint of tongue just below my clit, and I fear that I'll explode too soon.

"Another finger in my pussy, then, and a finger on my ass." I really can, I can have what I want, and it's hard to speak slowly, I'm so turned on.

"Squeeze my breast, too, my nipple, oh please," and there is a hand at my chest.

"Lick me, oh god, lick my pussy," I moan, and he does, as I rock back and forth, trying to rub myself against his face. I keep trying to touch him, any part of him, but my wrists are still clipped to my ankles and I can't. I still pull; I need the bite of the metal against my flesh to slow me down, to keep me from coming too quickly, but I can feel my body gathering up anyway. I breathe through my mouth again, my body heaving. It's hard to speak now, but if he just keeps doing what he's doing I won't need any more words, I can get there like this.

And then he pulls back, removing his hand from my breast and fingers from inside and mouth from my clit and moves back.

"All right, then, it seems you understand—" and I scream, loudly I scream, because this can*not* be happening, he can*not* leave me like this, he couldn't be so cruel, I will die!

"James fuck me please fuck me oh god you have to I need you please James fuck me fuck me I need you inside me you have to please please fuck me—"

I know I'm babbling incoherently, but I can't help it, I'm so desperate, I can feel hot tears running down the sides of my face, he can't leave me, he just can't, and then I feel his strong hands on my hips, his cock just at my entrance, and I am so there that as he enters me my orgasm is already starting, and as he pushes in it takes me in waves. He doesn't stop but slowly moves in and out, slowly fucking me as I come on him, my whole body convulsing arhythmically. My ears are ringing, I can feel my extremities, fingers, toes, even teeth, humming with the surge, as if every cell of my body has been flooded, electrified. The waves finally subside, my body stops rocking. I'm sucking in air as if I'll never get enough.

When I can talk again, I say to him, urgently, because I'm so afraid he won't know, "Please James don't stop don't stop."

He chuckles softly. "Don't worry, love, I have no intention of stopping now, I assure you."

With one hand still gripping my hip, he unclips my wrists from my ankles with the other. Oh, sweet relief! I stretch my bent legs out, I move my arm in circles as if I were tracing a snow angel, and then, oh yes, I can reach him at last, I can touch him. My hands and mouth are hungry for him, after being kept away so long, and I can't get enough. I kiss him urgently, face and mouth, and my hands go everywhere, his cheeks, his chest, along his back. I can't quite reach his ass, though I try—but I can cup his balls with one hand if I wrap my legs around him, angling myself and then pulling him so that he drives deeper inside me. I hang onto his back for support, digging my nails into his muscles. His breath is ragged, and then I feel his balls tighten and the vein underneath throb, and I know he is almost there. I sink my teeth into his neck so I can feel that moment from top to bottom, his shuddering into me. As he finishes, I squeeze him with my pussy muscles; I want every last drop inside me.

It's not hot, but we're coated with a sheen of sweat. He sticks to me slightly as he slides off to my side. I press against him, my head on his chest, listening to the thudding of his heart. His hand is on my head, possessively, protectively, his fingers playing in my hair.

"I'm your slut, James," I murmur.

"Yes, I know, Shar. You surely are." A pause. "You know, we wouldn't have to go through this if you trusted me, if you trusted us."

I don't know what to say to this. Is he waiting for me to say I trust him? Or to promise that I will in time? Or to explain why I can't? As if I actually had said something of this nature, I'm almost tempted to add a comment about how enjoyable it was, however, being taught my lesson—for both of us. And why not? Isn't the reassuring and the being reassured at least as fulfilling as taking and being taken for granted? If he has to claim me again and again, why should we choose to label that as some kind of obstacle instead of celebrating the motivations it gives us? With my eyes closed, it's easier to see. What brought me here, us here, isn't important, and there's no need to speculate about the future. I'm with him now. Here, in this moment, we are completely together.

Surely. With him. Now. Here. In this moment. Completely together.

Manner, purpose, place, and time. That's what adverbials are good for.

DEVIL'S NIGHT

Veronica Wilde

Ariel stood before her closet looking for her sexiest red or black dress. There wasn't much to choose from: the autumn night was chilly, and most of her dresses were on the skimpy side. But tonight she had to dress to impress, and her stomach jumped nervously as she reviewed her highest heels. Maybe she should just wear the red velvet halter dress and forget the cold. What did a little suffering matter when it came to impressing Tanner's friends?

She tucked a long chestnut strand of hair behind her ear and glanced at her boyfriend undressing for his shower. The classic tall, dark, and handsome, Tanner wasn't nervous at all, of course. Then again, they were his friends—and he'd been to play parties before. She hadn't.

He gave her an encouraging smile. "Don't wear a bra tonight, Ariel. And remember—the dress code is black or red. Devil colors." With that, he strolled naked into the bathroom, leaving her to admire the roll of his firm ass with a sigh.

Tonight was Devil's Night: the night before Halloween.
Tomorrow night they would pass out candy to trick-or-treaters.
But tonight they were going to a play party hosted by Tanner's
friends. When she was a kid, Devil's Night was the night the
neighborhood kids vandalized houses and yards. But tonight's
party would involve mischief of a more adult kind. An anxious
quiver went through Ariel as she took off her bra and slipped
into the red halter dress. In their two months together, Tanner
had helped her realize her fantasies of becoming a sexually submissive woman. Together they had explored the most
exciting and erotic nights of her life. But she had yet to meet any
of his friends, and she couldn't help wondering what kind of
tricks would happen tonight.

Her mind flashed back to the Labor Day barbecue where
she had met Tanner. He had been the tall, rangy, dark-haired
guy talking to the host. Right off she'd noticed the contrast
between his clean-cut good looks and the cool hunger in his
hazel eyes. He'd noticed her too, but despite exchanging several
challenging gazes, he never approached her. In frustration, she
slipped inside to visit the bathroom. Footsteps sounded behind
her in the dark hall, and she caught just a glimpse of his dark
hair before he took her hands, firmly gripped them behind her,
and forced her forward against the wall. She was too shocked
to say a word. Who did this kind of thing? His hot mouth found
her neck, his teeth grazing her skin. A dozen erotic wishes shot
through her mind like meteors—if only he would slide his
hands up her shirt to cup her breasts, no, wait, she wanted him
to put those hands under her skirt.

Instead he laughed, released her, and asked her on a date.
Over dinner, he'd told her what the host had said: *Ariel Banks
chews men up and spits them out.* She flushed as she admitted
that she had burned through a few boyfriends, but only from

boredom. They'd been nice, but they hadn't—excited her. She wanted a different kind of a man. She wanted...

"A dom," Tanner said.

Her cheeks burned. At last she had met someone who knew the language, knew what she wanted. Knew all the dirty things she wanted to be forced to do. "Right. It's just that I..."

"Aren't part of the BDSM scene and wouldn't even know how to meet someone who is."

She smiled shakily. "Okay, mind reader, what else do you know?"

"That you're going to go the restroom, remove your panties, then come back to the table and spread your legs just enough to give all those businessmen over there a good look at your pussy."

The fever of embarrassment and arousal had filled her whole body. As she got up to obey, she knew he was the man for her.

Thinking of their first date now made her shiver. She still couldn't believe that she'd finally found a man who worshiped her like a beautiful princess every day, then dominated her like a helpless slave every night.

The shower shut off. "Cold?" Tanner appeared behind her in the mirror wearing only a towel around his hips. His wet dark hair leaked rivulets down his sharp cheekbones.

"No. Just a little nervous about tonight," she admitted.

"Ariel." Without breaking their gaze in the mirror, he pulled down the front of her dress and stroked her nipples. "As long as you trust me, there is nothing to worry about. You do trust me, right?"

"Completely," she murmured, her blood firing as always beneath his touch.

The Devil's Night play party was hosted on the affluent side of town. Ariel was impressed as they pulled through a security gate and into a long circular drive. The brick house rising before them was old and stately, an October crescent moon just clearing the rooftop. A few dry leaves blowing across the lawn completed the scene.

"Remember, everyone here will know that you're with me," Tanner said. "If anyone asks you to do something you don't want, just say no. But I doubt that'll happen."

They parked and walked hand in hand to the carved wooden front door. The woman who opened it looked exactly like Ariel's idea of a dominatrix, from her black leather bustier to the leash in her hand. It connected to a young redheaded man who wore only a collar and a pair of jeans. "Oh, Tanner! Come in. And this must be Ariel. Don't you two look gorgeous. Come in, come in."

Ariel tried to look confident. So far the other guests seemed to be just chatting and drinking, all dressed in the requisite black and red. The massive living room was full of leather chairs and sofas, with a fire roaring from a stone hearth. The smells of perfume, leather, and burning firewood commingled pleasantly in her nose. So far this seemed like any party. Only the massive mirror on the wall opposite the fire hinted at the debauchery scheduled to take place here.

Then she noticed the topless French maid collecting empty glasses. Okay, so perhaps this wasn't like *any* party.

As if perceiving her thoughts, Tanner squeezed her hand. "Wine? Or do you want to keep a clear head tonight?"

"No, some wine would be great."

They went into the kitchen, where the dominatrix-hostess asked another topless maid to serve a tray of éclairs. She turned back to Tanner. "Help yourself to whatever you see. Although if you're in the mood for a real sight, I suggest you follow me—

Zach here is going to be punished for violating the dress code."
She smacked the leashed boy's blue jeans with a riding crop. He
winced.

"Not now, but thanks," Tanner said. "I want to take Ariel
around."

He guided her into another room. Here the crowd seemed
to be almost all men, their attention focused on the end of the
room. Ariel saw the object of their interest: a giant wooden
X-frame cross and the pale, black-haired girl shackled to it. She
was naked, her pink nipples stiff and her small breasts flushed
with arousal. A tall man in a black tux was flogging her, the red
welts contrasting with her snow-white skin. Though she was not
normally attracted to women, Ariel couldn't help admiring the
girl's body—and wishing for one jealous moment that she was
the naked object of adoration at this party.

She turned back to Tanner. To her amusement, he was
absorbed in a conversation with the host about cars. "Did you
even notice there's a naked girl in the room?"

He laughed. "Yeah, but I've already got a much cuter naked
girl of my own." He squeezed her bottom. "What I don't have
is a Jag and Mike here just bought one. Will you be okay if I go
take a look? I'll be back in a few minutes."

"Sure, of course." Leave it to Tanner to get excited over a car
at a play party.

Tanner and the host disappeared. Ariel wandered back to
the living room to get another glass of wine. Her butterflies
of anxiety weren't quite as fierce now, but she still wanted to
fortify her nerves for whatever surprises the night would hold.

Then she saw a ruffled blond head by the fireplace, and her
anxiety exploded into full-blown panic. Devin, the arrogant
bike messenger from her office, was here.

Oh god no, anyone but him, she thought wildly. In all her

worries about tonight, she'd never considered finding an acquaintance here. These people were experienced BDSM players, after all. But there he was with a beer in his hand, Mr. Insolent Flirt himself.

A dirty smile spread across his lips. "Ariel Banks," he said and sauntered over. "Well, well."

She felt her cheeks stain pink with embarrassment. Devin was a legend at her office, where he delivered packages several times a day. Twenty-four and boyishly cute, he was always cocky, always flirting with all the women in the office. His impudent smile said that he knew just how much they adored his visits. Secretly Ariel enjoyed the way his eyes lit up whenever she came out in her heels and suit to accept a delivery, but she always treated him coolly. She just didn't care for the way all the other women fawned over him.

And now he was at her play party. It was beyond mortifying.

"Happy Devil's Night," he said. "What are you doing here?"

"Oh, my friend brought me." She wondered if he and Tanner knew each other. "We're not staying long."

He brazenly looked over her clingy red dress and cascading hair. To her horror, she felt her nipples stiffen. She wished desperately she had worn a bra.

"Why not?" he asked. "You obviously knew the dress code. You must be here for the same thing as everyone else."

"No, we just stopped in," she lied.

Tanner poked his head into the room. "Ariel," he called. "I'm going to take the Jag for a ride. Be right back, okay?"

She nodded, and he left without so much as greeting Devin. At least they didn't know each other.

"Your date?" Devin asked.

"Yep." She drained her wine.

"Let me guess," he said, his blue eyes gleaming. "You're

going to be one of the topless maids tonight. Serving drinks and canapés in a French maid uniform."

"Of course not. Don't be ridiculous."

"Or maybe you like cracking the whip and you've got a boy tied up somewhere."

"Devin, would you just stop?"

"Or maybe what you really like," he pursued, "is being bent over and spanked in front of an audience."

Her face flooded with involuntary heat.

"Ah, so that is it," he said. "You want your dress lifted as everyone watches your beautiful ass get spanked—"

"Shut up!" she ordered and fled the room before he guessed at any more of her sexual secrets. This was a nightmare. What if he went back to the office and told her coworkers how kinky she was? Spying an empty laundry room, she ducked into it. But before she could compose herself, Devin was fast on her heels.

He shut the door. "Hey, I'm sorry if I upset you. I was just kidding around."

She shook her head. "It's okay. I just didn't want you to think..."

"That spanking gets you all hot and bothered?"

Goddamn him. She stared at the tiled floor, wishing he would go away.

Instead his hands slid around her waist. As he lifted her up onto the dryer, she knew she had to stop him. She was here with Tanner, after all. But Devin's masterful way of taking control blotted out all her willpower.

He pushed up her dress and stared at the scrap of fabric shielding her pussy.

"I think what you need," Devin said, "is to get warmed up with a different kind of spanking."

Oh god, no. Having her pussy spanked was even cruder and

more humiliating than a regular spanking. Yet she couldn't find the will to stop as he ordered her to hold her thighs open for him.

Face burning, she opened her legs. Lightly but firmly, he slapped her sex. The skimpy silk of her panties did little to blunt his fingers, and the tingle in her clit intensified. Her thighs strained open wider as Devin spanked her pussy again and again. She closed her eyes as she succumbed to the electrifying sensation of his fingers. Her nipples were so stiff they ached. Yet an inner voice reminded her that she was in love with another man. A devoted man who was probably looking for her right now.

"I can't do this," she whispered and jumped down from the dryer to bolt from the room.

The roaring fire in the living room seemed like the judgmental flames of hellfire as she returned. She fanned herself, desperate for fresh air. What was wrong with her? Not only had she betrayed Tanner, but Devin would never forget this. He would lord it over her constantly.

"Ariel. There you are."

Tanner strode in the front door with shining eyes. Even in her distress, Ariel couldn't help noticing how many of the women followed him with their eyes. Pride reminded her of what a gorgeous man he was; love reminded her of all of the tender, passionate nights he had given her. "You feel like making a store run? Mike said I could take the Jag to pick up ice and other supplies."

She forced a smile. "Sure." Maybe Devin would be gone by the time they returned. Better yet, maybe he would get blind drunk and forget that snooty Ariel Banks from the office spread her legs for him in a laundry room at a party.

As they drove to the store, Tanner rhapsodized about the car. "It's amazing. Like art meets machine. I know you don't care about cars but..." He went on so enthusiastically about the Jaguar that Ariel began to feel even worse. He didn't even suspect anything was wrong; that was how much he trusted her.

He pulled into the parking lot. "Be right back," he said.

She stared through the windshield, the full knowledge of her complicity weighing down on her. A flirtation was one thing; letting another man touch her was just wrong. Should she confess? She had promised to always be honest with Tanner, but he was a passionate, intense man. He might well break up with her on the spot.

Tanner came out of the store with two paper bags of tonic, ice, and food. "So what do you think?" he asked, patting the car's leather interior. "Should I get one when I win the lottery?"

She forced a smile. "Sure."

"Ariel...what's wrong? You've been acting odd. Did something happen at the party?" His hazel eyes were full of concern.

"No, not at all."

"Just tell me. Was someone rude to you? Aggressive?"

"Everything is fine. I'm just tired."

"Bullshit. Ariel—we agreed we would always be honest with each other. We have to be, with the kind of relationship we have. We're not like vanilla couples. We're playing on the edge and we need to trust each other."

She couldn't meet his eyes. She knew he was right, and yet she couldn't risk losing the only man who had captured both her body and her heart. Just this once, she thought wildly. I'll lie just once, and then I'll never do anything like that again. I promise.

She stroked his dark hair. "I do trust you," she said. "And I swear to you that nothing happened."

He looked hard at her. Then he nodded and started the car.

"Okay."

They drove back to the party in silence. She hoped fervently that he would hand off the bags, say his good-byes, and take her home. It was almost midnight, after all, and she'd said she was tired. And he seemed different himself as he guided the car through the leaf-strewn streets.

The party was still in full swing as they walked in. Tanner handed the bags to the hostess and turned. Ariel felt herself go pale with horror as Devin strode toward them. "So?" he asked Tanner.

Oh god. They did know each other.

"She lied." Both men looked at her.

No. This couldn't be happening. It wasn't fair. She loved Tanner, she hadn't wanted to lie, she had just wanted to save their relationship.

"I—how—" Her voice sputtered out.

Tanner casually steered her into a bedroom. Devin followed, shutting the door behind them. Despite her terror, a submissive thrill filled her at being alone with two such dominant, vibrant men.

"Ariel, meet Devin," Tanner said. "One of my close friends. Although obviously you two already know each other."

Shame glued her eyes to the floor. "I'm sorry," she whispered.

"Just listen," Tanner said. "When I told Devin I was dating a brunette named Ariel who worked for an insurance company, he figured out pretty fast that he already knew you. We share many things and sometimes that includes women. I hoped tonight that you might be attracted to him. But I also hoped you would be honest about it."

"You tested me," she said hotly.

"And you failed." He shrugged. "Look, I didn't tell him to touch you. But he texted me when I was in the store and I gave you an opportunity to be truthful. You lied."

Her stomach was knotted. "So now what?"

"So now you have a choice. Accept your punishment or go home—alone."

"Punish me," she said immediately.

"It will be a public punishment, Ariel," he warned. Both men watched her closely.

She hung her head so her hair shielded her burning cheeks. "Punish me," she whispered.

Ariel wobbled on her high heels as Tanner forced her to walk in front of him into the living room. Here the play party was fully underway with floggings, spankings, and other scenes everywhere she looked. Yet to her rising panic, almost everyone stopped to look curiously at her. *Of course,* she thought miserably, *I'm the new girl here.* Her head reeled as Tanner clapped his hands.

"Hello everyone. This is Ariel. She was dishonest tonight and you know how we all feel about that. So now she's going to be punished."

She stared desperately at thick dark carpet. She felt like an object, a sex doll displayed for everyone to see.

Tanner smiled deviously. "Darren, Mitch, put the footstool in front of the mirror. I want everyone to watch this but I want to force her to watch as well."

Watch what?

"Go lie down across the footstool," Tanner commanded and pushed her in front of him.

Catching sight of Devin's smirk, her first instinct was to protest. But she obeyed. The footstool was a wide black leather ottoman big enough to cradle most of her. She was aware of every eye in the room on her as she awkwardly knelt on the floor and lowered herself onto the leather until her arms and head dangled from one end, her ass and legs from the other. It was an undignified position, and the knowledge that cocky Devin was watching made it even worse. How could she ever face him in the office again?

Her panic intensified as the two men Tanner had called on bent over. One quickly cuffed her wrists together in black leather restraints while the other slipped her ankles into an iron spreader bar with two circular enclosures. It forced her legs apart until her red velvet dress strained tight against her thighs. Her face and bound wrists faced the mirror so she could see all of the guests gathering behind her. Her heart began to pound like a trapped animal's. What were they planning on doing to her?

Tanner spoke to someone else, who handed him a black leather paddle. Oh god no. Was he really going to spank her here in front of everyone? He spanked her at home of course, and she loved it, but that was different from being spanked in public as a punishment. Unable to stop herself, Ariel twisted helplessly on the footstool. "Tanner, please."

The first ringing slap on her bottom silenced her immediately. "Any further protests will result in additional blows," Tanner said in a severe tone. "Is that understood?"

She nodded miserably.

"Excellent."

She cringed, waiting for the next. Instead Tanner gently rubbed her ass through her dress, stroking her inner thighs. Abruptly, he pulled her dress up to her waist. She cringed, knowing everyone was looking at her tiny thong and thigh-high stockings.

"Well, now. Let's see what you showed Devin."

To her mortification, he slid her thong down her thighs and exposed her pussy to the entire room. Reflexively she tried to close her legs, but the spreader bar held them far apart. Her face burned with embarrassment as everyone crowded around for a closer look.

"Look at yourself in the mirror," Tanner ordered. "Don't close your eyes and pretend this isn't happening."

Ariel forced herself to meet her own gaze. Her face was a deep red, flushed with the arousal of such erotic and public humiliation. The unmistakable lust in the eyes studying her sent another bolt of desire through her. Unwillingly she noticed Devin's reflection in the mirror. That insolent smile taunted her as he took a long look at her pussy.

The second slap of the paddle took her by surprise. She bucked against it, and a third one came, then a fourth, as she twisted and howled in protest. Tanner spanked her a fifth time, and that tingling heat began to fill her blood. When the sixth blow came, she let it push her forward so her bare clit rubbed against the leather. Tanner spanked her again, and they fell into a rhythm, Ariel pushing her pussy against the leather as the paddle electrified her bottom. Heat spread through her body, stiffening her nipples and making her moan, until a stern hand grabbed her long hair.

"Stop that this instant," Tanner commanded. "This is a punishment, not a reward. You don't get to come until you're truly sorry for lying."

He spanked her again, holding fast to her hair. Just as she thought she'd go mad from frustration, he dropped her hair and began to play with her pussy. Casually his cool fingers drifted over her inflamed folds while she twisted and moaned, unable to stop. "Please," she whimpered. "Please, just fuck me."

"Do you promise that you will always be honest?"

"Yes, yes. I will always be honest."

"Honest about what?"

She forced out the words. "About what a wanton little slut I am." Helplessly she thrust her hips back at him, begging for his fingers, his cock, anything to fill her.

"You need to make it up to Devin too, Ariel."

Oh no. She wanted to fuck Devin, of course she did secretly, but not like this, not where he could take advantage of her helplessness and order her around. She would never be able to sign for a delivery again. But Devin was already kneeling in front of her face and unzipping his pants with a grin.

"Come on, you've wanted his cock for a long time," Tanner taunted her. "Now you're going to suck it right here in front of everyone. If Devin says you're good enough, you can come tonight. Otherwise..." He shrugged.

So Devin held all the power. Goddamn him. He laughed at her outraged expression and took out his hard, long cock. As he traced its swollen crown around her lips, a deep heat filled her pussy.

He tapped her mouth. "Suck me and do it right."

Taking a deep breath, she opened her mouth and he pushed himself inside. With her hands cuffed, she tried to suck and lick his cock as best she could. Tanner was still playing lightly with her clit, but she forced herself to concentrate on making Devin come without using her hands.

"That's right," he said. "Suck it like the dirty girl you are. Not so professional now, are you?"

Then Devin did what she hoped he wouldn't: unfastened the halter top of her dress and took out her bare breasts, playing with them until she groaned around his cock. Desire thundered through her body, and she knew she would lose her mind if they didn't let her come. Frantically she sucked Devin harder and faster.

He was breathing raggedly. "She's good," he said to Tanner.

"I say she can come."

Moments later, her master's thick, hard cock drove into her pussy. Ariel moaned as Tanner fucked her, raising her eyes to his in the mirror. This was one of her dirtiest fantasies, two men using her body in public just like the exhibitionist she always wanted to be. Devin pulled his shaft out of her mouth and slapped her lips and cheeks with it, while her ass and breasts bounced in rhythm with Tanner's thrusts. All three of them were groaning and shaking. Devin stroked his cock in front of her face, then pushed back in for the last strokes of her tongue. With a deep moan, he pulled out again and ejaculated all over her breasts and mouth.

Panting, Ariel looked at her reflection in the mirror, that submissive girl who was tied up, half-undressed, and covered with cum. Immediately she began to come herself, her pussy squeezing and throbbing around Tanner's cock. As her orgasm shuddered to a stop, he pulled out and flipped her over, thrusting into her mouth. Ariel swallowed every warm, salty drop of his orgasm as he tenderly stroked her hair.

The room broke into applause. She felt dizzy and almost high as Tanner and Devin helped her to her feet. She had really gone through with it: had been bound, stripped naked, and used by two men while people watched. Her first play party was glorious beyond her most exciting dreams. She snuggled into Tanner's side as he wrapped a protective arm around her.

"Let's get you home," he said.

A sudden sleepiness overtook Ariel in the car. She leaned against Tanner and watched the moon through the windshield. "Well, you made it through Devil's Night," he said. "Not bad for your first play party."

She looked up at him. "Will you share me with other men?"

He kissed her hair. "Possibly. But only your body. Never your heart."

She tucked her arm through his. "Never. I belong only to you."

At home they took a long, hot shower together, Tanner rubbing shower gel into all of her tired muscles. After toweling off, they climbed into bed. "Happy Halloween," he said as he pulled the sheets over them. "Get a good night's sleep. You'll need it."

She snuggled against his warm skin and frowned. "I thought we were staying home and answering the door for trick-or-treaters."

He grinned. "We might have a special trick-or-treater at the end of the night. But don't worry about that for now." He kissed her. "Sweet dreams."

Ariel drifted off to sleep in his arms, already blissful with the dreams she knew they would live out together.

ABOUT THE AUTHORS

JANINE ASHBLESS is the author of five Black Lace erotica books of paranormal and fantasy erotica. Her short stories have been published by Cleis Press in the anthologies *I Is for Indecent; Playing with Fire; Frenzy; Best Women's Erotica 2009;* and *Best Bondage Erotica 2011.* She blogs at janineashbless. blogspot.com

VIDA BAILEY is an aspiring writer in awe of those who manage to parent, work their day jobs, and still meet deadlines. She has published stories in Alison Tyler's *Hurts So Good* and Sommer Marsden's *Dirtyville* anthologies. You can find her at www. heatsuffused.blogspot.com

RACHEL KRAMER BUSSEL (rachelkramerbussel.com) is a writer, editor, blogger, and event organizer. She's edited more than forty anthologies, including *Spanked; Bottoms Up; Please, Sir; Please, Ma'am;* and *Best Bondage Erotica 2011* and *2012.* She is senior editor at *Penthouse Variations,* sex columnist for *SexIs* magazine, and covers sex, dating, books, and pop culture widely.

CLARICE CLIQUE has written a BDSM novel called *Hot Summer Days.* She has also had short stories published in various magazines, anthologies, and e-books including *Like a Queen* and *Sex in the City: London.*

Since hitting the number one spot in the U.K. erotica chart with her debut, *On Demand,* JUSTINE ELYOT has written extensively for publishers including Xcite, Cleis Press, and Carina Press. The villain is always her favorite character.

ANDREA DALE is a busy girl with stories in anthologies from Harlequin Spice, Avon Red, Cleis Press, and more. Still, she always has time for a bit of shopping.... Visit her at www.cyvarwydd.com and www.soulsroadpress.com.

KRISTINA LLOYD is the author of three erotic novels, including the controversial *Asking for Trouble.* Her short stories have appeared in numerous anthologies, including several "best of" collections, and her work has been translated into German, Dutch, and Japanese. Visit her at kristinalloyd.wordpress.com.

NIKKI MAGENNIS is a writer and artist who lives in Glasgow, Scotland. Her stories have appeared in numerous short story collections, including *Sex in Public; Sex with Strangers;* and *Sex and Music.*

SOMMER MARSDEN is the wine-swigging, fat-dachshund-owning, wannabe runner author of *Hard Lessons; Learning to Drown; Calendar Girl;* and *Lucky 13.* Her work has appeared in more than a hundred print anthologies, and her work has cropped up all over the Web. Visit her and her blog of chaos at sommermarsden.blogspot.com

EVAN MORA is a recovering corporate banker living in Toronto. Her work can be found in *Best Lesbian Erotica 2009; Best Lesbian Romance 2009 and 2010; Where the Girls Are; Please, Sir;* and *Best Bondage Erotica 2011.*

TERESA NOELLE ROBERTS writes romantic erotica and erotic romance for horny people who believe in love. Her short fiction has appeared in *Best of Best Women's Erotica 2; Orgasmic; Spanked; Best Bondage Erotica 2011;* and others. Her newest paranormal romance is *Foxes' Den.*

DOMINIC SANTI is a former technical editor turned rogue whose stories have appeared in many dozens of publications, including *Surrender; Yes, Ma'am; Caught Looking; Sex and Candy; Secret Slaves; Indecent Proposals;* and *Red Hot Erotica.* Future plans include more erotic short stories and a very irreverent historical novel.

SHARAZADE is professional writer, editor, and consultant who divides her time among Asia, Africa, the Middle East, and the United States. She enjoys stories that are realistic enough that they might have happened and fanciful enough that they might not have. She values communication, adventure, exploration, passion, and love.

Since leaving the small Idaho town where he grew up, **CRAIG SORENSEN** has spent his days working in information technology and his early morning hours pursuing his first passion of writing. His works can be found in numerous anthologies and publications. He can be found online at just-craig.blogspot.com.

DONNA GEORGE STOREY is the author of *Amorous Woman,* a steamy novel about an American woman's love affair with Japan. Her short fiction has appeared in *Passion: Erotic Romance for Women; Alison's Wonderland;* and *Best Women's Erotica.* Read more of her work at www.DonnaGeorgeStorey.com.

ALISON TYLER's (alisontyler.com) sultry short stories have appeared in more than one hundred anthologies, including *Sex for America, Liaisons,* and *Best Women's Erotica 2011.* She is the editor of over fifty erotic anthologies and twenty-five novels, including *Tiffany Twisted, Melt With You,* and *Something About Workmen.*

ALANA NOËL VOTH's work has most recently appeared in *Dream Lover; Bluestem;* the *Used Furniture Review;* and *Best of Best Gay Erotica 3.* Her story collection, *Fall,* is due in 2012. She likes red lipstick and green chili. Find her on Twitter and Facebook.

VERONICA WILDE is an erotic romance author whose books have been published with Liquid Silver Books and Samhain Publishing. Please visit her at www.veronicawilde.com.

ALLISON WONDERLAND (aisforallison.blogspot.com) has been writing erotic fiction and poetry since 2007. A do-as-I-say-knot-as-I-do kind of gal, she has written BDSM-themed stories for *Spank!; Hurts So Good: Unrestrained Erotica;* and *Sweet Love: Erotic Fantasies for Couples.*

KRISTINA WRIGHT (kristinawright.com) is an author and the editor of the Cleis Press anthologies *Fairy Tale Lust; Dream Lover; Steamlust;* and *Best Erotic Romance 2012.* Her erotic fiction has appeared in more than eighty anthologies. She lives in Virginia with her family and spends a lot of time in coffee shops.

ABOUT
THE EDITOR

SHANNA GERMAIN is a writer, editor, leximaven, wander-luster, and geek with a huge number of writing years under her belt (or her collar, depending on the day). Her award-winning erotic stories have appeared in more than two hundred antholo-gies and magazines, including *Best American Erotica; Best Bondage Erotica; Best Gay Erotica; Best Gay Romance; Best Lesbian Romance; Best Lesbian Erotica; Do Not Disturb; Please, Sir; He's on Top;* and more. She is the author of the forthcoming fantasy novel, *Between the Devil and the Deep Blue Sea.*

Her short stories, essays, and poems have garnered a number of awards and nominations, including a Pushcart nomination, the Rauxa Prize for Erotic Poetry, and the C. Hamilton Bailey Poetry Fellowship. In 2010, she was a finalist for the John Preston Short Fiction Award and a nominee for Best of the Net.

She invites you to explore the dark, dirty, naughty recesses of her mind at www.shannagermain.com.